He smiled and squeeze
made a soft exhaling s
over and flip on the
news. The duplex rou
feet per second, pierce
the safety glass where
startled girl panicked and hit the brake.

He groped furiously through his pocket and extracted an orange-tipped incendiary tracer round.

The girl stared through the perforated windshield as the car slowed down.

The bullet streaked orange down the length of the highway, passed through the license plate and found the gas tank. The beautiful Jaguar with the beautiful girl in it erupted into an orange ball of flames . . .

By the same author

The Hammer of God
The Smack Man

JACK CANNON

The Sniper

This edition published 1993 by
Diamond Books
77–85 Fulham Palace Road
Hammersmith, London W6 8JB

First published in the UK by
Grafton Books 1991

ISBN 0261 66211 2

Printed and bound in Great Britain by
BPCC Paperbacks Ltd
Member of BPCC Ltd

*NOTE TO THE READER

The Sniper was first published in August, 1974, by Nordon Publications/Leisure Books and was written by Nelson De Mille. Jack Cannon is a pseudonym for Nelson De Mille.

THE SNIPER

ONE

Henry Cyrus placed the rifle between his legs and knelt down behind the parapet of an abandoned five-story building that overlooked the FDR Drive. Behind him, the sun was setting into the Jersey cliffs; below him, a steady stream of traffic lurched its way up the Drive along the East River.

Cyrus rested his chin on the warm stone ledge of the parapet and stared into the gathering dusk. The flat, squat buildings across the river in Brooklyn looked deserted. As a tug pushed a barge of garbage downstream, a gigantic Pepsi-Cola sign uptown by the UN winked on and off. A chopper flashed across the sky, headed for the Thirty-fourth Street heliport.

"So many good targets," Cyrus said aloud. "More than in the jungle."

He thrust his hand into the pocket of his green bush jacket and removed a bottle of orange soda.

Slowly gulping the soda, he flipped a switch on his telescopic lens. Raising the rifle, he scanned the city with the Starlight Mark V scope, looking for a moving target.

He sighted in on the helicopter.

One thousand yards. Too far.

He looked up from the scope and rubbed his right eye. The sun had finally set, and the eastern sky was becoming dark. "A bad time to go hunting," he said to himself. "Old Starlight won't do the job for you, when Mr. Sun is still smiling."

Suddenly, his own smile faded. He saw the sleek outline of a Mercedes 560 SL convertible heading north along the elevated highway. He could just barely make out the long blond hair of its female driver streaming through the wind. He knelt upright; he searched through his pocket to retrieve a green-tipped duplex 7.62 mm round. He jammed it into the chamber and sighted.

One hundred yards and coming.

Through the scope, he could see the beautiful young woman smiling as she held up a candy bar and unwrapped it with her teeth.

Fifty yards and coming.

The Starlight scope gave the scene an ice-blue tint—face, blond hair, candy bar, car—all were different shades of blue. But even the uncomplimentary color couldn't hide this woman's good looks.

Abreast . . . passing.

The scope hairs crossed in the middle of the woman's head. Her long hair looked like a blue fire flickering in the wind.

Fifty yards and going.

He released the safety, took a deep breath and held it.

One hundred yards and going.

As she moved the car into the outside lane, he

swung the gun left to follow. The woman glanced at her watch. Eight P.M. exactly.

Two hundred yards.

He smiled and squeezed the trigger. The silencer made a soft exhaling sound and the operating rod slid back. He could hear every moving part of the rifle because of the silencer. The woman leaned over and flipped on the eight o'clock news. The duplex round, at a velocity of 2,800 feet per second, pierced two neat holes through the safety glass where her head had been. The startled woman panicked and hit the brake.

Three hundred yards.

Shit.

He groped furiously through his pocket and extracted an orange-tipped incendiary tracer round. He jammed it into the chamber and released the operating rod. The bolt slid home into the chamber.

The woman stared through the perforated windshield as the car slowed down; a stream of air blew into her face through the holes.

Steady now. Easy shot, easy shot.

Four hundred yards.

He drew a deep breath, guessed where the gas tank would be on the car, and fired.

Five hundred yards. Past the maximum effective range of the M-14 rifle.

The bullet streaked orange down the length of the highway, passed through the license plate and found the gas tank. The Mercedes erupted into an orange ball of flame and jumped into the path of an oncoming Ford Mustang. The Mustang caught the Mercedes in mid-flight and drove it over the guardrail to the street below. The flying car, landing on the roof of a passing van, started a chain reaction of destruction. The Mustang careened crazily southward and sideswiped three cars before it came to a stop against the rear of a truck and burst into flames.

The street below the elevated highway was littered with the dead and dying. The walking wounded stumbled around in a daze and collapsed beside the dead. The FDR Drive was a blazing inferno of hot steel; people were screaming and crying above and below. Traffic on the Drive began to back up in both directions. Horns blared and sirens started to whine through the still, hot August air.

Henry Cyrus leaned his elbows on the parapet and cupped his chin in his hands. He had never seen anything so beautiful in his life. This was better, so much better than the hospital. Better, even, than the jungles of Vietnam.

"You did a job on them people, Mikey," he said, stroking the rifle at his feet. "Want to take a few more pings down there, Mikey? No? Yeah. I remember what the Captain said, 'Zap and split—don't wait around for them to zero you.' "

As he glanced down at the carnage, his pale eyes blazed red, reflecting the fires below. It was as if a door in his head had swung open for a moment to reveal the fiery madness locked inside his brain. It lasted only a second, then his eyes became opaque again.

"Tomorrow's another night, Mikey. Tomorrow's another night."

He grabbed the weapon and the expended shells, rose quickly, and ran in a crouch to the roof door. He slipped through the door and quickly bolted it, never seeing the two frightened young teenagers peering down at him from an adjoining rooftop. "Hold me," the girl said, pressing her slim, naked body against her boyfriend's.

"Let's go," he whispered, wrapping his arms around her.

"No. I'm too scared," she said, running her hand down the boy's bare leg. "Let's wait."

Henry Cyrus moved as noiselessly as he could down the creaking stairs of the deserted building. As he reached the second-floor landing, he heard a noise. He didn't want to turn on the Starlight scope because he knew its blue glow would give away his position. Besides, he was too close to his target, and there wasn't enough light to power even this experimental scope. Remembering an old trick, he plastered himself against the stairwell wall and glanced sideways toward the foyer. Peripheral vision was much better than proximal vision at night. He smiled to think that his night fighter tricks were coming back to him. It had been a long time—more than twelve years.

As his vision improved, he could make out a swaying drunk urinating against the foyer wall. The smell and sound wafted up the stairs. Cyrus smiled again. *This is not your lucky day, bro.*

With a single leap, he cleared the last five steps and landed squarely on the foyer floor. The yellowed marble was already slick with urine and sputa. He slid, caught his balance, and pivoted, holding the rifle across his chest. The old drunk was still facing the wall, holding his penis, when Cyrus smashed the gun's butt against the back of his head. He sank noiselessly downward to his knees. His chin caught on the top of the wainscoting for a moment, and Cyrus brought the butt of the gun forward again with such force that it smashed the back of the old man's skull, pushing his face through the decaying plaster. The dead man became attached to the wall in that obscene position, still urinating. His brains and blood made an ugly fresco on the rotting plaster.

Cyrus quickly unmounted the scope and laid it on

the hall radiator. He loosened his baggy black pants and slid the rifle down, muzzle first, until the silencer caught in the top of his canvas and rubber jungle boot. Then he pulled up the loose-fitting jungle jacket and guided the rifle's butt into his armpit. Its forty-eight-inch length fit snugly there. He lowered his arm, pulled down his jacket, and walked stiff-legged to the radiator. From behind it he retrieved an old newspaper. He carefully wrapped the scope in the paper, then slowly he opened the outer door, looking up and down. The street was deserted.

"Everyone's gone off to the big fire, I reckon," he said aloud and smiled. The blood and brains on the gun butt felt warm and sticky as they mixed with the sweat of his armpit.

Henry Cyrus whistled as he walked away from the sirens and screams.

TWO

Detective Sergeant Joe Ryker, New York City Police Department, sat on a bench in Tompkins Square Park on a sweltering August evening. If anyone could have looked through the Porsche sunglasses he wore they would have seen an ocean of contempt in his green eyes. Most men couldn't eyeball Ryker for more than a split second. As their eyes dropped self-consciously to escape his disturbing stare, they would quickly pass over the rest of his grim face until they rested on a safe spot around the area of the necktie. Later they would remember the thin aquiline nose and expressionless mouth that had registered in their subconscious with uneasiness.

The East Village, Ryker thought. That's what they began calling it in the late 1960s when it was bursting at the seams with kids from comfortable Long Island suburbs playing hippie. It was a long-haired, pot-smoking, grabby-feely, pimply-faced version of Haight-Ashbury, a pre-yuppie Disneyland where you could get stoned, get laid, get away from Mom and Dad and discuss politics with a real, live Negro. It was peace and love, a piece of ass, a piece of cake for the dropouts, draft resisters and dipshits who wanted to be a part of the revolution without going all the way to California.

It wasn't the radical 1930s chic of the real Village, then called, condescendingly, the West Village, with its corps of faggot-faced old dudes in baggy pants discussing Marx, Mahler and Mahatma Gandhi. No, this was the place for bell-bottoms, bra burnings and boo; of Herman Hesse, Peter Max and crash pads. It was cheap, crummy and chaotic, but it had love, man. It also had junkies, desperados, murderers, rapists and a whole contingent of mentally ill who may have been crazy, but they weren't stupid: They knew where the handouts were. So did the drunks who migrated up from Houston Street. In the Bowery, they were considered scumbag nuisances; in the East Village, they found fame and an occasional meal as local characters, real street people, tourist attractions.

All this couldn't go on, and didn't. By the early 1970s the Hell's Angels moved in and the nice boys and girls from Great Neck and Scarsdale began to move out. The war in Vietnam was winding down, and law school looked a lot better than a smelly loft crammed with eighty-six horny teenagers. Crabs and the clap were just not something you messed with in your twenties. So by the mid-1970s, the East Village had sunk back into its pre-hippie drabness, a working class neighborhood filled with Ukrainians, Spanish, and hold-out Eastern European Jews who hadn't left their apartments since 1906. The drunks drifted back to Houston Street, the junkies continued to make new converts and the old neighborhood sank into a catatonic decline—waiting.

Ten years later the waiting was over: The yuppies were coming, the yuppies were coming. Gentrification—the day of the well-heeled locusts was at hand. Rat-infested firetraps were being converted into luxury condos; vampire real estate magnates were rounding up the squatters and driving them out; the beloved alkies of the '60s were being set on fire or hounded out of the neighborhood; surprised illegal aliens were suddenly being carded; and the street people were encouraged to find new streets to trash with their presence.

The East Village is more or less a rectangle, a mile long on one side and a half-mile wide, depending on where you set the boundaries. No one knows how many people live there, since the residents don't hold honest and informative discussions with census takers. Who's going to tell *La Migra* that your forty-two cousins are up from Colombia and living in the kitchen, or that your whole village in Jamaica is now staying in a neat row of cardboard boxes in your basement?

The northern boundary is roughly Fourteenth Street, a fashionable shopping district some hundred years ago, now a drug peddler's paradise. The neighborhood ends down at Houston Street on the south, where it abuts the Lower East Side, former home of pushcarts, peddlers and half the rich rag merchants in town. On the east is the River, East River Park and the FDR Drive. And on the west the Demilitarized Zone's Third Avenue or maybe Fourth Avenue; it's hard to tell where the boogie stops and the woogie begins.

Smack in the middle is Tompkins Square Park, a delightfully green refuge in the crumbling neighborhood. The green, of course, is mostly moldy dog shit mixed with wino vomit and junkie spit. A rotten place to visit, and you wouldn't want to live there.

"Look at them," Ryker said, motioning at the passers-by with a lazy sweep of his hand.

The young man sitting next to him had been doing just that for the last hour. Patrolman Arthur Hayes, originally from Montauk, New York, at the tip of Long Island, but now of the New York City Police Department, thought he knew what trouble looked like, but he was doing a lot of new thinking right now.

Still looking straight ahead, Hayes said, "Joe, I thought I had seen it all working Queens, but this little sideshow you got here is one strange . . ."

"Yeah," Ryker said, allowing himself a thin smile. He liked this young man as much as he was capable of liking anyone. Because he liked him, and because he was a professional, he meant to fill this country boy with as much of his experience and knowledge as possible before the kid asked for a new partner, which was only a matter of time.

Hayes was what they called a "silver shield"—a patrolman working temporarily as a detective. Two years on the force as a uniform had earned him a chance at a detective slot. His two years, however, had been spent in the relatively peaceful suburb of Queens. Manhattan was the big leagues, and Arthur Hayes wasn't quite prepared for it. Knowing this, he had kissed his wife and kiddies good-bye in their Queens condo and taken a cheap hotel room near the precinct until he could get his feet on the ground. Ryker, whose working day sometimes stretched for twenty hours, approved.

Ryker decided that a complete tour of the precinct was a good way to begin Hayes's new assignment, and for the last two days and nights they had been walking and bar-hopping, sight-seeing and scumbag-rousting.

They had walked the perimeter of the area, then Ryker had shown him the crack houses, drug dens and shooting galleries that dotted the area like poppy seeds on a roll. He had explained to Hayes that Avenue A was *the* place for heroin, while Avenue C always had the cleanest and sharpest needles. You had to know shit like that to be a successful junkie. Or a successful cop.

Ryker had shown him the middle-class project to the north of the East Village: Stuyvesant Town is filled with relatively affluent white people paying 1940s rents. He had shown him the Lillian Wald Houses, the low-income project at the other end of the boundary. These people didn't pay much rent either, but they had a better view—and smell—of the once-blue East River. They had a better view because they had knocked out most of the windows in the buildings.

Ryker had pointed out hookers, pimps, junkies, speed freaks, alcoholics, vagrants, homosexuals, transsexuals, transvestites, lesbians, exhibitionists, and just plain criminals. He pointed out a black man, completely naked, taking a shit in the middle of the street; he broke up a fight between two armed, toothless bag ladies; he had had to put on his sunglasses to avoid blindness as the junkies flashed their needles in the bright sun.

The people here were black and Spanish, both homegrown and Caribbean; whites from every national background in Europe; Asian Indians and American Indians; Orientals and nondescript hybrids; Yankee Americans. Many citizens of this modern Babylon sported native costumes: long flowing robes, saris, turbans, caftans, fezzes, and dashikis.

"Is this America?" Hayes mused. "Did I catch the wrong subway out of Queens?"

Ryker was indifferent. He had long since stopped concerning himself with externals.

A blond teenaged girl wearing a skimpy red sundress had been sitting opposite them on a bench, staring vacantly into space. An equally young, fresh-faced kid crossed the park and approached the girl. She nodded toward Ryker and Hayes. Ryker caught the words, "fuck 'em," from the kid. She put a finger to the side of her nose, then held out two fingers in a V-for-victory sign. The boy nodded and she followed him out of the park.

"There goes twenty bucks worth of crack," Ryker said.

"She made a buy right in front of us?" Hayes asked.

"Nobody gives a fuck anymore." Ryker shrugged, but he was slightly outraged by the balls of that bitch, copping like that in front of them.

Hayes watched the pert young ass of the girl as she crossed the park. There was a lot of naked flesh around on this ninety-degree night. Short shorts, bare feet, bare backs and bare bellies. Ebony black flesh, chocolate flesh, ruddy flesh and pale white flesh. The skin, the heat and the rumbling vibrations from the passing traffic had created a lazy sensuous feeling in Hayes's loins. He remembered he hadn't seen his wife in two days.

"Come on, champ, let's get," Ryker said, standing. "Orientation class is over."

"Mighty fine ass," Hayes drawled, still staring. He seemed to stand up in sections, his long gangly body bending and unbending, stretching and scratching. Both men pulled at their crotches and seats.

"B.V.D.s rode clear up my asshole," Hayes said seriously. "Major wedgie."

Ryker looked distracted. "This fucking heat is loony weather. The full moon doesn't help either. We got homicide weather, Arthur, not humpin' weather."

Ryker removed his sunglasses, wiped the sweat

from his face, and began walking toward the south exit of the park. Hayes fell into step beside him with a few lanky strides.

"What happens now that orientation and terrain appreciation is over, Joe?" Hayes asked. "You taking a vacation?"

Ryker laughed; it wasn't a funny sound. "I've got work to do," he said. "I've got cases up the ying-yang and you're going to help me with them. They aren't much to write home about because none of them has attracted much attention from the press, the Commissioner, the neighborhood, and, least of all, me. Run of the mill assaults, robberies and murders—one prostitute, one junkie, one vagrant, and a little family argument that ended in the decapitation of somebody's uncle or brother-in-law."

"Decapitation?"

"Machete. Folks were from Haiti or some damned place down there. Strictly PDU stuff," he said, referring to the Precinct Detective Unit that investigated local crimes.

"Oh."

"Well, what's it going to be—some chow or some pussy?"

"Pardon?"

"You've been lugging a hard-on around like it was a terminal tumor."

"Oh."

"Okay, any way you want it," Ryker said. "I don't mind pimping for you, now that you're in the Big Apple, but I'm not going to stick it in for you, too."

"We're on duty, Joe," protested the young man. "Besides, I'm married."

"Three cheers for duty and marriage," Ryker said. "Let's eat."

They walked west on Seventh Street until they came to First Avenue, then went into a sidewalk café called Victor's. The waiter recognized Ryker and nodded but made no move to seat him. Ryker looked up and down the line of patrons who were seated at the best tables next to the glass enclosure facing the sidewalk. He strode quickly up to two customers who were in deep conversation over a pitcher of sangría. Ryker removed his gold badge from his pocket and tapped it on the marble-topped table. The younger man looked up and said, "Oh, shit."

"Pipe down, Percy," Ryker said quietly. "I just need your table."

Before either of them could answer, two waiters appeared and began moving the glasses and pitcher to an interior table.

"Fascist," hissed the older man as they moved off. Ryker sat down, lit a foul-smelling cigar and put on his Porsche sunglasses. Hayes stood uncertainly for a few seconds, then joined him.

"Who were those guys?" he asked.

"A couple of scumbag armed robbers who were probably planning a job," Ryker said. "They should do their work in some dark back room, not a table with a view."

"I guess," Hayes said, picking up a red velvet menu with the words VICTOR'S—CUBAN CUISINE stamped in gold on the front. "Nice place," he said appreciatively, glancing around at the plants that gave the glass enclosure a greenhouse effect.

"Since you don't approve of where I usually eat, it's your treat, sport," Ryker said. He usually ate only hot dogs and hamburgers. Sometimes pizza, if he couldn't find hamburgers or hot dogs.

"My treat and my pleasure, Joe," Hayes said expansively, wondering how far his money would stretch if they were going to repeat last night's bourbon guzzling.

A smiling waiter approached and bowed. *"Buenas noches,* Sergeant Ryker. Besides a nice cold beer, what may I bring you?"

"A hamburger," Ryker said, without glancing at the menu.

"May I recommend . . ."

"Recommend nothing, Sebastian. I only come here for the view."

"Certainly."

"My friend here, though, is a connoisseur of Cuban cooking."

"Is this so?" the waiter asked, turning appreciatively toward Hayes, who was trying to decipher the menu.

Hayes looked up with a start. "Well, now . . . I think. . . . Say, is this like Mexican food?"

"Make it two hamburgers and two beers, Sebastian," Ryker cut in.

"Sí," the waiter said as he gathered the menus and stamped off.

The hamburgers and beers came. They ate and drank in silence. Ryker watched the world slide by and thin out as the hour got later. He never tired of this carnival.

"I was just thinking," Hayes said between bites of overcooked hamburger, "about that little broad in the park. The blonde."

"Yeah?" Ryker said before draining his third bottle of Carta Blanca beer.

"She was kind of cute."

"She's flyin' by now," Ryker said, burping. "A cracked-out crack. She's thinking about her next score."

"Don't kids ever screw anymore?"

"Yeah, but they like junk better. Fucking a junkie's like fucking a dead fish," Ryker said, wiping his mouth with the back of his hand.

"Great!" Hayes said, smiling.

Ryker had to look up to see if he was joking. You could never tell what they did out there in the country.

THREE

Ten minutes later, Ryker edged slowly into the restaurant's hot, fetid phone booth. He dialed the precinct and asked to speak to Detective John Littel. After a few slow rings that seemed as though they were affected by the heat, Littel picked up the phone.

"Got anything for me?"

"Glad you called, Joe."

"That so?"

"Listen, there's been a hell of an accident on the Drive, sector twenty-one bravo."

"I can hear the noise from here, and I hope everyone's having a good time, but what the fuck's that have to do with me?"

"All available personnel to the scene. Fischetti's orders. Some witnesses said the whole mess started when a car blew up on the Drive."

"Maybe it was struck by lightning."

"C'mon, Joe, this may be big. Besides, the whole world is there now."

"Okay, okay. Can I stop home for my Brownie? My mommy likes to see pictures of where I work."

"It's a real mess, Joe."

"Right. I'll have to settle for the official pictures, but they're always in black and white."

Ryker hung up and went out to the street where Hayes was waiting. He was annoyed with this assignment because it didn't look very promising.

"Got anything, Joe?"

"Follow the big red fire truck," Ryker said as he moved off in the direction of the noise. After two days with Ryker, Arthur Hayes was used to short, unenlightening answers, so he shrugged and followed.

Ryker hailed a passing patrol car, flashed his tin, and he and Hayes jumped in the back. The two young patrolmen knew Ryker by reputation and didn't seem too happy having him as a passenger.

They rode in silence the remaining few blocks. As they approached the police barricades under the elevated highway, Ryker and Hayes jumped out. They shouldered their way through the crowd and passed through the barricades with a wave from Kenny Schneider, once the fattest cop on the force. Schneider had spent fifteen years waddling around Yorkville, the German-populated section of the city and never passed a restaurant without inspecting its kitchen. When he topped three hundred pounds, he was transferred downtown where the Department hoped that the Spanish, Italian, and soul food would disagree with him. It did, and his weight dropped to two hundred and fifty pounds. Ryker walked over to him. He always got background material from an older patrolman before he faced the brass.

"*Buenos días,* Mr. Patrolman. Can I interest you in a hot tamale . . . arroz con pollo . . . chili?"

"Fuck you, Joe."

"Be nice, Kenny," Ryker said, patting the patrolman's stomach.

"Fuck off," Schneider said, pulling away.

"Who's here?" Ryker asked.

"Take a guess."

"What are my choices?"

"Well. A: the Commissioner himself, for starters; B: every politician who wants to get elected or re-elected in November, from the dogcatcher on up—or down, depending on how you look at it; C: the brass, including Captain Peterson; D: all of the above; or E: none of the above."

"I guess 'D.' But why?"

"Lots of bodies, lots of fire, lots of newsmen. Possibility of foul play. That sort of thing."

Ryker turned to Hayes, who was surveying the wreckage. Emergency Service vehicles, ambulances, fire trucks, and police cars were everywhere. All of the seriously injured had been taken to Bellevue Hospital, and most of the bodies had been taken to the medical examiner's office next door to the hospital. As the fires ebbed, the Emergency Service personnel began to cut the living and dead from the twisted wrecks. Police and fire searchlights whirled around dizzyingly; figures moved like phantoms through the broken illumination; popping flashbulbs gave the scene an unrealistic quality.

"It smells like shit," Hayes said absently.

"Roasting flesh. Make you hungry, kid?"

"What was it, Joe? A bomb?"

"No. Seems a car did a double gainer off the Drive."

Hayes looked upward. "So?"

"So they think the car blew first," Ryker said,

looking around. "Can you find the brass, kid? We gotta report in." He moved toward the center of the disaster area.

"Go where most of the bulbs are popping, Joe. You taught me that."

Ryker smiled. "You're going to make a good detective, kid."

Both men were smiling as a flashbulb popped in their faces. Ryker was blinded, but he lunged instinctively for the photographer. The man disappeared behind a fire truck.

"Well, if it isn't Joe Ryker, crimebuster," said a voice dripping with sarcasm.

Ryker blinked hard. He knew that voice. So did millions of other New Yorkers. It belonged to Craig Rogers, New York's top local TV newscaster, who had suddenly thrust a microphone in front of Ryker, even before he could utter the "fuck you" that was on his tongue.

"Excuse me, Sergeant Ryker," Rogers said in a deferential tone for the microphone. "What do you think caused this terrible tragedy?"

Ryker was fuming. Through his flashbulb blindness, he could just make out the ghostly specter of a TV camera trained on him.

I owe you one, motherfucker, Ryker thought.

"Sergeant Ryker?"

"Yes, Craig," Ryker said with forced civility. "I was off duty and in the neighborhood when this tragedy occurred, so I thought I'd stop by to see if I could help out."

"Very commendable, Sergeant," Rogers said, an edge of mock surprise in his voice.

Scumbag, Ryker thought.

"Sergeant Ryker? Sergeant Ryker?"

Ryker looked up. He had apparently missed a question.

"Sergeant Ryker, is there any truth to the story that the car that started the chain reaction blew up before . . ."

"I just got here," Ryker snapped. He strode off in the direction of a fire truck whose ladder reached to the elevated highway above.

"I didn't know you were so popular with the working press, Joe," Hayes said.

"Rogers and I have different ideas on how I should do my job."

They stopped by the burned-out shell of a Mercedes 560 SL convertible next to the ladder truck. The car was upright, but it showed signs of having been tossed around quite a lot before it found this resting place. Inside, still sitting behind the wheel, was a charred human form.

"Seat belt must have burned away after the car came to rest," Hayes said.

The Crime Lab had roped off the car and were starting to go over it. Ryker walked over to a fireman standing at the base of a ladder. "Anything good up there?"

"Depends on what you call good, Mac. Lots of big shots and brass. The mayor, too. He missed some kinda society ball or somethin'—he's still in a tux. Probably pissed."

"Well," Ryker said, starting up the ladder, "this looks more interesting than a cotillion."

The fireman just grunted.

"Stairway to the stars," Hayes said.

When Ryker and Hayes reached the top of the ladder, they climbed over the guardrail and faced the East River. A small breeze was starting to blow in from offshore; both cops drank in the cooler air for a few seconds.

"Smells like a cow's asshole, but it sure as hell beats flesh and tires," Hayes said.

People from the country have strange expressions, Ryker thought, as the two cops walked across the highway toward the large knot of dignitaries and press people on the other side. The highway was a shambles, but a single lane had been opened in each direction for traffic. Cars were backed up for miles in either direction. A fire department "cherry picker" was lowering the wounded to ambulances below where the local traffic was thinner. Captain Carl Peterson spotted Ryker and pulled away from the crowd.

"Glad you could make it," Peterson said.

"Looks like King Kong got loose again, Captain," Ryker said.

Peterson was a tall, thin man about forty-five years old, with stringy blond hair and washed-out blue eyes. His face showed the scars of adolescent acne. As a long-time crony of Chief of Detectives George McVey, Peterson had spent twenty years working at police headquarters, shuffling papers and writing memos. But McVey was grooming him for higher command and decided to send him out into the field for a little practical experience. He had headed up three special task forces that had each solved a highly publicized murder. In each case, Peterson appeared before the cameras to take the bows; in two cases, it had been Ryker who had done the work.

"You going to head up a new task force on this, Captain?" Ryker asked.

"Perhaps," Peterson said. "It depends on . . ."

"On how much time Craig Rogers devotes to this," Ryker cut in.

"Ryker . . ." Peterson started to get angry but

thought better of it. *I need this arrogant asshole,* he admitted to himself.

About a half dozen of the police brass had pried themselves away from the civilians from the mayor's office and drifted over to Peterson.

"Joe, you know everyone here," Peterson said. Ryker didn't, but responded in the affirmative. Hayes, ignored, smiled self-consciously.

"Can you run it down for me, Captain?" Ryker said in his most professional manner.

"Of course, Sergeant," Peterson responded in kind. "It seems this Mercedes was heading north. . . ."

"The one roped off below?"

"Yes, and at least four witnesses who survived the ensuing wreck have stated unequivocally that the automobile blew up as it was traveling in the left lane before it hit anything."

"It didn't look like a high-explosive type bomb from what I saw of the wreck."

"No, it was obviously the gas tank that went."

"Could have been a mechanical malfunction of some type? Dragging muffler . . . leaking gas tank?"

"The Crime Lab is going to do a post mortem on the car. We're only speculating for now."

"Okay. Small detonator on the tank?"

"Could be," Peterson said in a noncommittal tone.

"Mafia or political?"

"We don't have a make on the driver, yet."

"Why on the open road? That would suggest an odometer-connected or time bomb. Too risky—might get the wrong person. Might get nobody," Ryker said.

"Maybe radio controlled. Planted right in the road or in the car. Signal given from a rooftop."

"A little farfetched, Captain, considering all the simpler types of bombs available."

"We'll know a little better when we get a make on the victim and a Crime Lab report on the car."

"What's taking so long with the make?"

"Everything is ashes, including the driver."

"License plate?"

"No evidence there ever was a front plate. Out-of-state car, probably. Back plate appeared to have been blown or knocked off, according to the preliminaries."

"Are we really sure the Mercedes didn't hit something first?"

"Four witnesses, Ryker," Peterson said, with a trace of impatience. "Probably more when we get through with the hospitals."

Ryker reflected a moment. "Let's talk to the witnesses."

"They're dry, Joe."

"Not until I squeeze 'em, Carl."

Peterson shrugged and pointed to a small knot of people standing in one of the closed lanes. "Okay. They're all yours."

Ryker turned and started toward them. Captain Peterson excused himself and followed Ryker; the brass walked back to suck up on the mayor and the Police Commissioner.

Hayes found himself standing alone. His first impulse was to follow Ryker and the captain, but he was already too strained by the supercharged atmosphere Ryker seemed to generate wherever he went. He'd had enough of this strange man for a while, so he wandered over to talk to a group of patrolmen who were picking up odds and ends from the pavement for the Crime Lab.

Ryker stood staring at the motley group before him. They looked tired and scared.

"Five."

Peterson looked at the group. Three men, a woman and a little girl of about six or seven.

"Okay, five," Peterson said, wearily.

"Everybody driving in separate vehicles?"

"Except number five," the captain said.

Ryker approached the mother and child. "What's her name, ma'am?" he said, trying to make his disturbing eyes seem friendly.

"June—Junie. Please don't give her any more candy or junk, officer—she's had her fill of it from everybody else."

Ryker hadn't considered giving the child anything. He didn't know much about children, except what he saw on an occasional TV show. His ex-wife had laughed when he had suggested they have a baby. "One of you is enough," she had said. *One of her was enough, too,* he thought.

Ryker knelt down beside the little girl. "What happened tonight, Junie?"

"The cars wrecked," she replied, edging toward her mother.

"Did you see the little car, without the top, wreck, too?"

"It was yellow."

"The little car?"

"Yes. It had a pretty lady."

"Driving?"

"Yes."

"Did you see her up close?"

"I waved when she passed."

"The pretty lady in the little yellow car—she passed you?"

"Yes, and she waved back."

"Then she was ahead of you?"

"Yes, then she slowed down."

"Then what happened?"

"The orange stripe followed her."

"Orange stripe?"

"It was fast, like in *Star Wars.*"

"Star Wars?"

"Like the space rays."

"Like the lasers in the space movies—it followed the small yellow car with the pretty lady?"

"Yes."

"Ryker, the child . . ."

"Shut up, Peterson," Ryker growled. He turned back to the child. "Did the orange ray hit the car, Junie?"

"Yes."

"Then what happened?"

"The car blew up."

"The yellow car with the pretty lady?"

"Yes. It blew up. Is the pretty lady dead?"

Ryker stood, looked up and down the highway, and said, "As a doornail."

FOUR

It was a little before eleven P.M. when Ryker finally found himself in front of his apartment on East Ninth Street. The day had started for him at seven A.M., when he routed a hungover Hayes out of his hotel room. Ryker climbed the four flights of stairs to his walk-up apartment in a fading brownstone, built in a simpler, more gentle age. He sprawled in front of his TV set and switched to Craig Rogers's channel for the eleven o'clock local news. It had been a long day, but it was always satisfying to make an ass out of Peterson. Unfortunately, when something satisfying like that happened, there was always the piper to pay, Ryker thought, and he knew he would start paying in the next few minutes.

The TV camera focused on Craig Rogers mouthing words about "the tragedy on the east side." After giving a body count, which had risen to fourteen killed and thirty-six injured, Rogers's face disappeared and was replaced by a film of the grisly scene.

This particular station never spared its viewers anything, which is why it was the most popular news source in New York. Rogers himself narrated the film that focused on burnt and mangled bodies; nude and half-nude men and women were seen being helped into arriving ambulances.

They got there before most of the police, Ryker thought.

Rogers's face was back after a good minute of the ghoulish film. He wore a look of concern and sympathy.

". . . and our deepest sympathy to those who . . ." he droned on.

"Sure," Ryker said aloud, "after showing everyone maimed, burnt and naked—you bastard!"

The camera panned backward, and a large screen appeared behind the commentator's head.

"Here's the zinger," Ryker groaned.

A picture of Ryker smiling materialized behind Rogers's head. It was the picture taken while he and Hayes were joking about the brass. Hayes, at least, was mercifully out of the frame. Ryker groaned again.

"We don't know why Sergeant Joe Ryker is smiling amidst all this suffering, while our fellow citizens burn, but we can only assume . . ."

"Fuck you, Craig."

". . . a filmed interview with Sergeant Ryker."

The film showed Ryker, as he knew he must have looked, blinking the camera's flash out of his eyes, staring stupidly into the microphone thrust under his nose.

"The old blitz." Ryker sighed. Flashbulb in the face, microphone in the nose, cameras and questions before you can scratch your nuts. Oldest newscaster trick in the book. And he had fallen for it.

Ryker stood up and snapped the set off. "I owe you one, Craig. I owe you a big one."

Ryker moved toward the phone and considered taking it off the hook. He knew it wouldn't be long before the reviews started pouring in. On cue, the phone jangled loudly in the quiet apartment. It was Arthur Hayes.

"Joe, did you see . . . ?"

"Yeah, Arthur, meet me tomorrow at the station house, seven A.M. sharp."

"Right."

As soon as he replaced the receiver, it rang again.

"Ryker here. Yes, I saw it," he said, without waiting for the query.

"Listen, Ryker," Peterson's voice came on the phone, "the Chief has decided to handle this as a homicide. I'm in charge, and since this is in your precinct, I want you on the case."

"To help you get you your deputy inspector's oak leaves?" Ryker asked.

"Shut up and be there at eight A.M. sharp. I'll set up my command post in your precinct," Peterson said.

"What a fucking pleasure it will be to work with you again, Captain. I can't tell you . . ." Ryker began, but Peterson hung up.

Ryker slammed the phone down. As soon as it hit the cradle, it rang again.

"Yeah?"

"Joe? Is that you?"

"Oh, hi." It was Eleanor, his ex-wife. She called every few weeks for some reason known only to herself.

"How's the brassiere account going?" he asked, tucking the phone under his neck and patting his pockets for a cigarette. He realized the call could take a while. Eleanor had an annoying habit of talking about people he had never met as if he was supposed to know them.

"The tampon account," she corrected him. "The agency is billing almost twenty million on that account, and I'm in charge."

"No shit," he said. *So what?* he thought. He could never figure out why she got so hot and bothered about selling a bunch of junk to the American public.

"No shit," she said, laughing. "And if I can nail down those pantyhose guys from North Carolina, I'm up for senior VP."

"Pantyhose guys," Ryker mused. He finally found a stale cigarette in his pants pocket and lit it. It burned the hell out of his lungs and he coughed.

"I told you to give those things up," Eleanor said. "They'll kill you." Though he knew she was calling from Chicago, she sounded like she was next door.

"Probably," he said, hawking up a wad of phlegm. "If the scumbags don't get me first."

"Stay tough, Joe," she said. "That's all you've got."

"Yo, Ellie. You call up to break my balls or what? 'Cause if you did, lemme get my answering machine on so I can record your sermon. That way I can play it back at my leisure and learn from your vast wealth of . . ."

"Phil said you'd react that way," Ellie broke in. "Defensive and surly, just because I try to stay in touch with you."

"Who the fuck is Phil?" Ryker asked, the anger in his voice apparent.

"You know, I told you about him. He's a guy I work with. Anyway, we were having lunch with Alice and Renaldo when you came up in the conversation. So I told them all about you and they said . . ."

Ryker let her yammer on about people he didn't

know or care about, expressing their opinions about him and his life. It was better than talking to reporters. But not much.

"Well, I'm glad to hear about your promotion and the brassiere account," he said after a few minutes. "But I've got to run."

"Tampon," she said automatically, then added, "at this hour?"

"At all hours," he said. She had never understood his *need* to be on the street, the high he got from working. That's why she had left him: He wouldn't move to Chicago when her agency had promoted her. Ryker lived with her for ten years, and when she had announced that her career was more important than their marriage, he had been crushed. He loved her, he thought, but he really didn't know her.

As soon as he had said good-bye and hung up the phone, it rang again. He let it ring as he walked into the bathroom and washed the soot off his face. His beige wash and wear suit was streaked with filth and smelled of burnt flesh and rubber, but he didn't notice or care. He moved into the bedroom, opened a dresser drawer, and removed a three-cell flashlight. From the top of the dresser, two smiling faces stared out of a plain picture frame: his own and Eleanor's. She was dressed in a brown tweed suit he liked because it made her reddish-gold hair shine like a halo. She was beautiful, intelligent, and a tiger in the sack. Ryker could never believe his luck in attracting and holding her. He was right about that.

He turned the picture frame face down on the dresser and went into the small kitchen, grabbed a bottle of beer and a few doughnuts and carried them into the street with him. The telephone continued to ring in the empty apartment.

Ryker walked east on Ninth Street, then south, then east toward the river. He didn't really know what he was looking for, but the idea of a sniper interested him. For Ryker, snipers were nuts who came in three distinct varieties: kids with new guns, professional assassins, and all-out loony-tunes. The first two categories didn't worry him. If a lucky shot had caused the incredible amount of damage, the kids and professionals would be running scared. A loosely wrapped shitbucket of a psycho, however, might have gotten his rocks off tonight and decide that he liked to watch the pretty fires and listen to the wailing sirens. That worried Ryker. A lot.

He was nosing around the crime scene, when a sudden movement made him go for his piece.

"I surrender," a voice from the shadows said. It was Bo Lindly, a detective from Ryker's precinct.

"What brings you out after dark?" Ryker asked.

"Come on, I'll show you," Lindly said, starting down a deserted street.

"I'm only interested in one thing tonight," Ryker said, following him.

"Yes, I know; this may be part of it. Did you know that your buddy, the Queens commando . . ."

"Hayes?"

"Yeah, Hayes. He found the Mercedes license plate after you left. It had what appears to be a bullet hole in it. No make on the driver, yet. The TV and radio news is panicking everybody with the old 'mad sniper' routine."

"Figures." Ryker was right about the sniper; he hoped he wasn't right about the psycho.

Lindly bounded up the crumbling steps of a deserted tenement. On the door was a police padlock and a sign:

POLICE CRIME SCENE
KEEP OUT

"Tell me you found the sniper screwing his rifle in here and he got his dick caught in the chamber," Ryker said.

"Close," Lindly said, opening the padlocked door.

Both men stood in the foyer and switched on their flashlights.

"Crime Lab and Forensic have finished up and the body's at the ME's. Old man—wino probably. Pissing against that wall. Head smashed in."

"Rifle butt?"

"It would appear so. At least two blows. Lateral and horizontal, not on the top of the head but at the back. Large blunt instrument. Sounds like the way somebody would use a rifle butt. 'Horizontal butt stroke' they called it in the army."

"Who found him?"

"The cheering gallery that came through here to see the fireworks on the Drive. Somebody got around to reporting it after they'd been on the roof about an hour. Everybody said they thought somebody else had called the cops. We chased them off the roof, but any traces of our marksman friend have probably been obliterated—if this was his perch."

"He could have used this opening to get to any roof along this block," Ryker said, looking around.

"Not likely. The roofs on both sides are a story taller. Can't get access without an accomplice to give you a boost."

"Did you give the roof a toss?"

"Well, yes, but there's so much shit up there. . . . We'll give it a fine-tooth at daybreak."

"Come on, this hallway stinks. Let's go topside."

Both men trudged up the stairs to the roof. They stepped carefully through the debris of many an illicit party. They could see empty whiskey and wine bottles, white and festively colored condoms, beer cans, glassine envelopes that had once held heroin, empty crack vials, and a few half-smoked joints.

"Wanna party?" Lindly asked.

"Not in this fucking hole. We'll come back at first light. Give me a boost onto that roof, then you can take off if you want."

"How are you going to get down if I go?"

"How am I going to get down if you stay? I'll jump. Now boost me up and make sure you leave the bolt open."

Ryker killed his flashlight.

"Okay, hard ass, up you go."

Ryker tumbled over the adjoining parapet while Bo Lindly left quietly.

Ryker crouched with his back against the parapet and listened. The moon had disappeared behind gathering storm clouds. He could smell his own body over the hot, tarry odor of the roof. On the far side of the roof he heard a low whisper, then his eye caught a movement. He slid his .38 Police Special from his ankle holster, then reassuringly touched the .357 Ruger Magnum under his armpit. He dropped into a prone firing position and bellowed, "Freeze—police!"

He could hear a whimper. Springing up, he crossed the roof in a few long strides. There, huddled against the opposite wall, were two sleepy-eyed, Spanish kids. They were both stark naked. Their brown, glistening bodies contrasted sharply against the white blanket under them. Ryker snapped on his flashlight.

"Well, Romeo and Juliet. *Hablan inglés?"*

"Sí," answered the terrified boy. "Let us get dressed, please."

"Stand up."

The boy stood, slowly followed by the girl.

Not more than thirteen or fourteen, Ryker thought.

The girl assumed the classical position of the surprised nude, covering her pubic region with one hand and her breasts with her arm.

"Let her get dressed," implored the boy. "She is only a kid."

"Kiddies don't fuck on the roof, only big girls do. Let's answer some questions first." Ryker kept his gun trained on them. Terror, he knew, was the best way to loosen a tongue—short of outright violence. "How long have you been here?"

"Since the people left. The people who watched the accident."

The girl nodded.

They seemed resigned to their humiliating position and wanted to answer as quickly as they could to get it over with.

"Not before?"

"No."

Ryker, catching an evasive look in the girl's eye, swung the flashlight in her face. He then moved the light up and down her naked body. She looked as if she wanted to back through the stone parapet.

"Bullshit! Stand up straight," Ryker barked to the squirming girl.

She began crying, silently, but Ryker was unmoved.

"You were here before the accident," he continued in a low voice. "You came to fuck when the sun was going down."

The girl looked wide-eyed through her tears.

These kids must think they're the only ones in New York who ever screwed on a roof, Ryker thought.

"Yes," the girl whispered, wiping away the tears and

trying to cover her small, unformed breasts with her elbow at the same time. "We came up like you said. A man on the other roof . . . we looked down . . . see him . . ."

The boy cut in. "He had a gun. We were scared, so we just hid up here."

"You saw him shoot."

"No."

"What did he look like?"

"We only saw his back. Tall, anglo, with the yellow hair."

"What was he wearing?"

"The green Army shirt."

Ryker thought a moment. He decided they were still holding out. *They don't want to say they saw the actual shooting,* he thought. Time to divide and conquer.

"Okay, sweetheart," he said, motioning with his gun. "On the other side of the roof. Move."

She glanced at the boy for a second, then began to run to the other side of the roof, her small feet making a shuffling sound across the gravel. The boy made a move.

"You stay right here, hero. If she makes with the right answers, she won't get hurt."

Ryker walked quickly to the opposite side of the roof, slipped the .38 in his pocket, and grabbed the trembling girl by her long black hair. He forced her down on her knees and began his questioning in a low, rumbling whisper.

"You saw this man shoot the gun?"

"No."

"How many times did he shoot?"

"We ran. We didn't see."

"What did the gun look like?"

"Long, very long." The girl was writhing on the sharp gravel. She tried to take some of the weight off her knees, but the more she moved, the more the gravel dug in. Finally, in desperation, she clutched at Ryker's legs and picked her knees up a few inches, balancing herself on the tips of her toes. Ryker forced her down again.

"Was there a noise when the gun fired?"

"We did not see him shoot."

The girl began to sob uncontrollably. Ryker loosened his grip on her hair and told her to stand. He strode to the opposite side of the roof where the boy was looking anxiously in their direction.

"Okay, your girlfriend spilled the *frijoles.* Now let's have your story, and it had better be the same, or I'll be using your *cajones* for tennis balls. *Sabe?"*

"Okay, I'll tell you everything," the boy said, dejectedly. "We saw him shoot."

"How many times?"

"Two, I think."

"You think?"

"The gun made no noise. The man went back like this." He pantomimed the jerking retort of a gun.

"No noise?"

"No noise."

"A flash? A fire from the end?"

"No noise. No fire. I thought I was going deaf, but the second time he shot, a long, orange flame came from the gun."

The boy told all that he could remember, and when he had finished, Ryker walked him to the parapet overlooking the deserted tenement. The girl was huddled against the wall. She made a pathetic attempt to cover up again as they approached.

"No time for false modesty, missy. Let's go. Over the top." He motioned to the roof of the tenement below.

"Hey, we told you everything—let us get dressed, huh?" the young boy pleaded.

"Move!" Ryker snapped.

The boy went first. Ryker grasped the kid's slim wrists and hung him from the parapet, then dropped him. The girl went next and was caught by her lover. Ryker followed in a single leap.

On the sniper's perch now, Ryker walked them through the scene of the crime again and again, step by step. He made notes with a well-chewed pencil stub.

"And this is exactly where he was kneeling?"

"Yes."

Ryker produced a dirty, gray piece of chalk and made a mark.

"Do you remember anything else about the man?" Ryker asked.

Neither kid spoke.

"How about the gun?"

"Well, there was that blue light," the boy said.

"Blue light?"

"Yeah."

"The light from the gun—you are sure it was blue, and not red or green?"

The boy nodded.

Ryker was puzzled. Infrared scopes gave off a red light; Starlight scopes, green. He made a note to check with ESU. They were the experts on exotic weapons.

"Anything else you can remember?"

"No."

The girl seemed to have overcome her shyness or didn't care anymore, Ryker noticed. He produced a pack of cigars and offered them around. A small gesture, but the boy accepted one self-consciously. The girl smiled and shook her head. Ryker lit both cigars and looked at his for a long moment. He turned to the couple, now sharing the cigar.

"Did he smoke? Did he drink anything? Eat anything? Think hard."

They thought. They were used to obeying this frightening man by now. He seemed to hold all the cards.

"Yes," began the girl slowly. "He drank an orange soda."

"Go on."

"He took it from the big pocket of the Army shirt and drank it."

"You're sure it was orange?"

"Yes. I was very hot. It made me thirsty to watch."

Ryker trained the flashlight on the rubble-strewn roof.

"Did he drop it here?"

"Yeah. He didn't finish it; he put it down."

Ryker bent over. In the beam of his flashlight was a half-finished bottle of Orange Crush against the parapet wall.

Ryker took their names and their addresses, which were in the projects nearby.

"Can we go?" the boy asked.

"Yeah. Beat it," Ryker said. But they stayed put, looking up at the formidable ten-foot wall that separated them from their clothes. Ryker walked over to the wall and locked his hands to form a stirrup.

"Let's go," he said.

The boy thrust his bare foot into Ryker's hands and was boosted over the wall to the higher roof. The girl hesitated, then raised her leg. Ryker could see the damage the gravel had done to her knee and leg. As he eased her up slowly, she blushed red through her creamy skin and smiled into Ryker's eyes. The boy grabbed her outstretched arm, and she was gone over the parapet.

Ryker noticed a tugging sensation in his groin as he bent over and stuck his finger in the neck of the Orange Crush bottle.

FIVE

The storm had broken, and Ryker was sopping wet as he stood facing the Saxon Hotel on East Third Street. He looked down at his watch. Twelve-thirty A.M.

There was nothing Saxon about this decaying structure: the facade was Italian Renaissance; the lobby, Spanish or Moorish; the help, all Spanish and black; the guests, seedy; and the night manager, Jewish.

He learned from the desk clerk that "Mr. Hayes has an overnight guest." He shrugged at the information and took the key, anyway. Crossing the lobby of threadbare Oriental rugs and dying palms, he wondered if he couldn't use a "guest" himself, about now. The security guard, a rat-faced rent-a-cop, was wondering the same thing, and he made Ryker an offer.

"Maybe later," Ryker said.

"Can I get you a fresh bottle of pop, chief?" the anemic-looking man asked sarcastically, as he looked at the sticky bottle of Orange Crush dangling from the end of Ryker's finger. "Say, maybe you'd rather have a boy," he continued, following Ryker into the urine-soaked elevator.

The elevator stopped at Hayes's floor, and the doors opened. The security guard was still smiling when he saw Ryker's green eyes boring through him. Then pain and darkness. Ryker stepped into the hall before the elevator doors closed on the doubled-up man. Ryker was raw and edgy and needed a drink.

He entered Hayes's unair-conditioned room. A fan spun lazily by the window. Hayes and a young, long-legged blonde were laying naked on top of the sheets, asleep.

Ryker walked over to the bed and grabbed a bottle of Fleishmann's gin from the night table. He took a long pull, gargled and spit. Then he sat on the bed next to the blonde and took another pull, which he swallowed. The figures on the bed stirred. Ryker snapped on the night lamp.

"Vice squad," Ryker said, through a ginny burp.

Hayes shot upright and the girl squealed, trying to cover herself.

"Funny how a pro gets shy when another man walks into the room," Ryker said. "Reflex action, I guess."

Hayes rubbed his eyes. "Joe?"

"No names, please. I've got a reputation to consider."

"Joe, what the hell . . ."

"I want to congratulate you on finding that license plate, Arthur."

The girl had worked herself under the covers. "What the hell's going on here, Artie?"

"Official police business, ma'am," Ryker answered solemnly. He took another long pull of gin.

"This could have waited till morning." Hayes said angrily.

"Could you get off the bed, please: you're all wet," the prostitute piped in.

"It *is* morning and, no, I can't get off the bed. I'm too tired." The gin was swimming around Ryker's brain now. The young whore giggled.

Hayes flushed. "Listen, Joe . . ."

"No, you listen. Number one, why wasn't the night latch on? Number two, where's your gun? Number three, you didn't leave a wake-up request at the desk. Number four . . ."

"Okay, okay, I was tired, too."

"That kind of tired could cost you, kid. If I were this bitch's pimp, I could have walked in here and walked out with your gun, your money, your badge, and your self-respect in my hip pocket." The blonde looked at Ryker approvingly.

"Run off and powder your nose, blondie," Ryker said. He had not missed the look.

The girl slid her long legs out of the sheets, rolled over Hayes and disappeared into the bathroom. *Bleached blond,* Ryker thought.

"What kind of telescopic sight glows blue?"

"What?" Hayes was slipping back into grogginess.

"Blue."

"How the hell would I know? Some kinda fancy Starlight scope?" Hayes asked. Then it dawned on him. "That what the son-of-a-bitch sniper use?"

"With a silencer and flash suppressor. What kind of rifle would it be, Arthur?"

"Well, shit—let me think. Probably the old M-14. That's what they used as a sniper rifle in Nam. Seven-point-six-two millimeter. Old, heavy, but very accurate. Not like this plastic shit they got today."

"Does it fire an incendiary tracer?"

"Sure. Where did you get this lead?"

"Romeo and Juliet. Kids screwing on the next roof. Listen, I want you to find out all you can about snipers, rifles, scopes, and all that stuff. Meet me at eight A.M. sharp."

"Okay, Joe. Goodnight."

Ryker ignored the remark. "Take this soda bottle uptown right now and get it dusted. Absolute priority. I want answers in eight hours. Melt the fingerprint computers if you have to."

Hayes groaned. Ryker could hear the unmistakable sounds of a douche being used in the bathroom.

Ryker ripped a piece of paper from his pad and threw it on the bed. "This is all we have for a description. Tall, blond, Anglo. The prints came from the right hand, although there may be some from the left hand and possibly other prints on the bottle. This guy may be clean up to now, but I suspect an ex-military type, so the Feds should have some possibles from their Armed Forces files. If they can't get a positive make from the prints, I want a list, with pictures, of all the maybes."

"Right."

"It's raining out, so be careful not to smudge the prints."

Hayes was up and dressed when the girl, wearing a towel, came back into the room. He approached the soda bottle on the dresser and hesitated.

"Stick your finger in it, Arthur."

Hayes shrugged and did as he was told.

"I'll take care of everything here. See you at eight."

With a backward glance, Hayes left the room and rang for the elevator. The doors opened, and the anemic security guard stared wide-eyed at Hayes from a sitting position. He saw the same Orange Crush bottle hanging from Hayes's finger, but this time decided not to mention it.

Ryker, meanwhile, was stepping out of his clothes for the first time in almost eighteen hours.

"Artie paid me for the whole night, so there's no charge to you, honey," the hooker purred, dropping the towel.

"Aren't you sweet."

"Real tough guy, huh?"

Ryker bolted the door and picked up the bottle of gin. He drained off the remainder and tossed it aside. The young prostitute suddenly looked scared. Ryker was naked, except for one sock, his ankle holster and gun. The girl was staring at the gun.

"You're really a cop, aren't you? I mean you're not going to hurt me or anything?"

Ryker picked up the towel and threw it toward the wide-eyed girl.

"Wipe me down," he commanded. This would have to do. He was too tired and horny to shower. The girl obeyed silently. When she was finished, Ryker ordered, "On the floor."

"The floor?"

"I don't stutter, baby."

The blonde got down on the dusty carpet and spread her shapely legs.

As he mounted her, Ryker smiled. "Didn't you ever screw on the roof when you were a kid?"

Five A.M. Ryker was in one of the greasy all-night coffee shops that dot Manhattan's lower east side. The storm had passed, and the air hung heavy with a clammy fog. A few vagrants sat huddled over cups of bad coffee. Ryker ordered his second cup, and the Greek behind the counter decided that Ryker was a cop or a criminal. As he put the cup of tepid coffee in front of him, Ryker flashed his badge. Cop. The counterman waited for the worst.

"What's your name?"

"Demetrius."

"I could have guessed. Listen, Demetrius," Ryker said, taking a chance. "A man came in here about nine-thirty last night. Tall, blond hair, wearing a green Army bush jacket. He walked with a stiff leg."

Ryker paused and searched the Greek's eyes. They were as cold and expressionless as his own. A tough guy, Ryker decided. The pause became a long silence. The two men held eye contact.

Finally, the Greek looked away. "Nope."

"Blond, tall, Army bush jacket?" Ryker repeated.

"Nope."

"You own this place, Demetrius? You can't make much dough here, but you'll make a whole lot less if I take you down to the station house. I'm a real busy man. It might take all day."

"Last night, yes. But about seven—seven-thirty," Demetrius said hurriedly. "He had something wrapped in a newspaper."

He wouldn't bring the gun into a public place, Ryker thought. He'd ditch it somewhere or he might live around here. Came here before he went hunting.

He questioned the Greek for fifteen minutes, threw a ten-dollar bill on the counter and left. He felt certain this man would be able to pick out a picture.

Ryker walked slowly toward the sniper's perch. Bo Lindly would be there shortly with some people from the Crime Lab. Ryker sat on the crumbling steps of the old tenement and lit a cigar.

The streets were deserted, except for a derelict who

was searching through the garbage cans before the sanitation truck arrived.

"The early bird gets the worm, Grandpa." Ryker's voice split the still morning air. The derelict looked up with a start. He didn't like what he saw and crossed the street. Ryker followed.

"Come here, old timer."

The old man figured he was in for a beating and a rolling at best, so he turned his pockets inside out to show Ryker that he had nothing on him. Ryker looked at the bum for a moment and wondered which of them looked seedier. He took his cigars from his breast pocket, pushed one into the old man's toothless mouth and lit it. The derelict smiled.

"You a cop or somethin'? A private dick?"

"Where do you sleep?"

"All over. Over there, sometimes." He pointed to the padlocked building. "Rooms are all locked and nailed, but I sleep in the hall or on the landings. They killed Charlie there last night."

"You know about that, do you?"

"Only that he's dead, mister."

"Were you friends?"

"Bums ain't got no friends. I only knew him."

"Ever see a tall, blond guy—wears an Army shirt?"

"What's all the big hullabaloo about a bum? They kill us every day, and all the cops usually do is haul away the body. Sometimes they don't even do that."

"This is 'Be Kind to Derelicts Week,' old man, so we're making a special effort. Answer the fucking question."

"I saw him once, yesterday. He was hanging around the block here."

"What time?"

"Mister, I haven't looked at a watch or clock in years."

"About?"

"Six, I guess. He was trying doors."

"Would you recognize a picture?"

"I guess so."

Ryker pulled a twenty-dollar bill from his pocket and ripped it in half.

"The other half will be at the Eighth Precinct about six tonight," he said as he stuffed the torn bill in the old man's shirt pocket. "Find yourself a public clock and be on time. You got a name?"

"Bob Reid."

"Ask for Ryker, Bobby."

The sun was filtering into the canyons of Manhattan. Coming up the sun-dappled, filth-strewn street, Ryker spotted Bo Lindly.

Lindly looked unusually chipper, considering the hour.

"Morning, Joe. Find anything good in the garbage pails or did the competition beat you to it?" He smiled, motioning toward the derelict. The bum was working frantically to keep ahead of the garbage truck, which had already begun its appointed rounds at the head of the block.

"Did you sleep on the roof last night?" Lindly continued.

"Did you ever screw on the rooftop when you were a kid?"

"No, I was raised in the suburbs. All the roofs were sloped. Only squirrels screwed on the roof."

"Let's go up top," Ryker said. "I have a good story to tell you before the Crime Lab gets here."

At seven-thirty Ryker mounted the front steps of the East Sixth Street station house. The East Village roughly corresponds to the Police Department's

Eighth Precinct. Two hundred and fifty cops operated out of the old roach- and rat-infested station house built in 1898. It was added onto in 1954, so the west wing of the building was in white brick rather than red brick. Actually both color bricks were now black with soot and pollution, achieving an unintended harmony.

Ryker nodded to the desk sergeant and walked upstairs to the second floor where the Precinct Detective Unit worked. The conference room, with its cigarette-scarred wooden table and filthy gray industrial carpeting, would be Captain Peterson's command post for the investigation.

Peterson wasn't in yet, so Ryker had the honor of chasing the roaches away from the coffee set-up. There was leftover coffee from the night before, so Ryker plugged in the electric pot. Tired, he sat in a creaky chair and lit his last cigar. As the coffee began to boil, Ryker poured himself a cup of the sludge, which he cut with fly-specked sugar and yellowed cream. Peterson strode in and glanced at Ryker. He didn't like anyone's getting to work before he did.

"Make yourself comfortable, sit down, light a cigar, have a cup of coffee," Peterson said, with mock politeness. The Captain did not like people who made themselves comfortable in his "command post," even if it wasn't really his office. Ryker knew this and didn't care. In fact, that's why he did it.

"That was a nice piece of interrogation on that little girl last night," Peterson said, grudgingly. "No one thought to question her. Of course, after Hayes found the license plate with the bullet hole, we would have come to the same conclusion. Also, it turned out that some of the witnesses in the hospital saw the trail of the tracer round."

"Got anything else?"

"Well, believe it or not, they found the slug among all that debris at first light this morning."

"Seven-point-six-two millimeter?"

Peterson stared at him. "I just found out five minutes ago."

"I found out earlier this morning."

"What else do you know? It's obvious from your appearance that you didn't stay home long after I called last night. Did Craig Rogers give you insomnia?"

"Sort of. Look, Captain, do you mind if we continue this discussion when Hayes gets here? He's supposed to meet me soon, but he probably got delayed uptown."

"Uptown?"

"The Academy. I had him bring some prints there last night."

"What kind of prints?"

"Later."

"When do you sleep?"

"During your briefings, Captain."

Peterson got up and walked to his door. In the squad room, four detectives were drinking coffee. Yawning, Lieutenant Fischetti had just walked in.

"Could you gentlemen come in here, please?" Peterson called. "We're going to start a briefing shortly."

The four detectives and Lieutenant Fischetti dutifully filed into the conference room. Ryker smelled as gamey as he looked, so the men avoided him as they sat down around the table.

"Gentlemen, some or all of you may be involved in this sniper business before it's over, so I want you here for this briefing. We're waiting for Hayes now and four more detectives I've got on a steal from Midtown

South." The men fidgeted as they made small talk. Only Ryker dared smoke; he had switched to cigarettes, a sure sign something was about to happen.

A little past eight A.M., Hayes, carrying a thick manila envelope, burst breathlessly into the conference room. "The prints were good. We have some . . ." He looked at the seven pairs of eyes staring at him.

Ryker spoke first. "Come in, Arthur, we're having a Tupperware party. Need a lettuce crisper?" Hayes walked in and sat on the coffee table.

"Let's begin," Peterson said sharply. "First, the driver of the Mercedes turned out to be a student at Columbia University. She was from Pennsylvania, no known enemies, et cetera. We can only assume she was a random victim. Probably the flashy car attracted the sniper."

Peterson went on rehashing and recapitulating endlessly. Ryker yawned. It was getting hotter in the closed office. Fischetti got up to open the window. It was stuck. Ryker took the manila envelope from Hayes and started to flip through the papers inside.

Peterson wound up his monologue and looked around the room. "Well, that's it, gentlemen. Does anyone have anything to add? Any suggestions on how we should proceed from here?"

Ryker waited to see if anyone wanted to speak. Peterson turned to him. "Do you want to let us in on anything, Sergeant, or are you self-employed now?"

Ryker stood up. Peterson flinched noticeably. Ryker always got the impression that Peterson thought he was going to hit him. One day he would be right.

Ryker finally spoke. "I don't think Bo Lindly has had a chance to report in yet, but you might remember that he caught the squeal on that dead derelict last night. It turns out his case is related to our little problem."

Ryker told briefly of his night wanderings, leaving out exact details of his questioning of the Spanish kids. He ended the story with the Greek, the derelict, and Bo Lindly.

There was a long pause as everyone collected his thoughts. Hayes was trying not to grin; Lieutenant Fischetti and the four detectives were impressed. Peterson was looking for a way to belittle Ryker's night's work.

Peterson broke the silence. "Why didn't these kids come forward earlier?"

Ryker sneered. "Look, Captain, about the same time kids in this city stop believing in Santa Claus, they stop believing in the system, cops, and everything else. A kid, from where you live, on the Island, would probably report . . ."

"Okay, Sergeant. I don't need a sociological discourse on growing up in the slums. These kids—I assume they were—ah—fornicating or something—and I assume you were less than gentle with them—would they make credible witnesses? Would they even testify again under 'normal' conditions? Why didn't you bring them here to make a formal statement? The same goes for the diner owner and the derelict."

Peterson was hitting his stride now. The other detectives shifted uneasily in their chairs.

Peterson continued, "Why did you sift through that rubble on the roof yourself? You could have called the Crime Lab back."

Ryker wondered again how this man got to where he was. Hayes, feeling the strain, began to sweat. Fischetti was planning on ways to intercede if Ryker blew up. After all, he was Ryker's regular commanding officer, an impossible job that he hated.

Peterson kept after him, making sure he mentioned Ryker's "interview" with Craig Rogers and a slew of other details about Ryker that had obviously been bothering him for months. He stopped abruptly in the middle of a tirade and slumped in his chair. A silence hung in the stifling room. Fischetti was spring-loaded, ready to step in between Ryker and Peterson if necessary. But Ryker sat down. Everyone seemed relieved.

"So, as I was saying, it looks as if we might have our man here in this envelope," Ryker continued, as though Peterson had said nothing. Peterson sat listlessly in his swivel chair, staring into space. "Arthur?"

Hayes jumped up.

"Tell us what you got uptown," Ryker said, handing him the manila envelope.

"Right. What I have here is files of people whose fingerprints might be the ones we found on the soda bottle that might have been handled by the sniper. I had to bust ass to get them so soon. The prints, unfortunately, were not all that clear. There are two hundred and eighteen possible suspects here—City, State and Federal. Now, the Federal is both criminal and military, since that is what we asked for. City and State are only criminal, of course."

Hayes paused and looked at Ryker. Ryker gave him an almost imperceptible nod. Fortified, Hayes continued. "For starters, we might want to put aside the files of those whose physical descriptions don't match 'tall and blond,' although we shouldn't discount them altogether. Okay, next, the out-of-town police departments will check on the status of anyone we request. Ninety percent will probably wind up all present or accounted for. We will check those whose last known address was New York City. We and the FBI will put special emphasis on veterans, since a military rifle was involved. I think that by this time tomorrow, we should be down to a couple dozen possibles. We'll be notified by phone as they start discounting these suspects." Hayes drew a deep breath. "Any questions?"

Ryker and Hayes fielded a score of questions from Lieutenant Fischetti and the detectives. Peterson was still staring blankly at the ceiling. The men seemed excited about this possible breakthrough.

Ryker took possession of the files again and continued to flip through them. "The telecopied pictures are only temporary, of course. When we get down to our 'possibles,' we'll get glossies from the appropriate agency. I should also point out that none of the MO's match this sniper routine. I really think that this guy is going to turn out to be an ex-military type. Does anybody want to comment?"

Everyone noticed that Ryker had taken over the meeting and that Peterson was either sulking or in a catatonic trance.

His reverie was broken by the arrival of the four detectives on loan from Midtown South. They shambled into the oven-hot conference room with the arrogance of gunfighters casing a hick-town saloon.

"You're late," Peterson snapped, sitting bolt upright in his chair.

The four detectives stared at him, then sat down at the end of the table, as far away from Peterson as they could get. One of the newcomers, Detective Sergeant Ralph Fletcher, a bald little man of fifty, rubbed his scalp and said, "Right."

Ryker laughed; everyone else tried to find interesting objects in the room to inspect.

Having already been put in his place by Ryker, Peterson decided he'd better shut up and get on with the case. He was a busy man and had a lunch scheduled with the Chief of Detectives. If these SOB's wouldn't respect his rank, he'd find some way to screw them. Every cop had his weaknesses and Peterson was expert at finding and exploiting them. He'd bring them into line—or break them.

Peterson then launched into another one of his interminable recapitulations, this time incorporating Ryker's information with his own. When he was finished, he asked for comments.

"Sounds like we've got this scumbag in our pocket," Detective Fletcher said, wiping the sweat off his glistening skull. "But I got a question to ask Ryker."

"Go ahead," Peterson said.

"How come you look so shitty?" Fletcher asked.

"Workin'," said Ryker. "Something you wouldn't know anything about, you sawed-off, baldheaded little fuck."

Fletcher laughed, a grating *haw-haw-haw* that sounded like an asthmatic wheeze.

"Gentlemen, please," Peterson said. "This is getting us noplace."

"But, Captain," Fletcher said. "He's stinkin' up the whole room. Request permission to open the window and throw him out."

Ryker flung a pencil at Fletcher, who dodged and began *haw-hawing* again.

Peterson was shocked. He felt he was dealing with a bunch of rowdy juvenile delinquents, not veteran detectives. He knew the dicks in the field were sometimes a problem, but *this* was absurd. What he didn't know was that Ryker and Fletcher had once been partners and had been going through this ritual for fifteen years, whenever they met. It was a game, a way of communicating for two men who had absolutely nothing to say to each other.

"Okay, everybody get out of here," Peterson said,

beginning to detail assignments. But he was interrupted by Ryker, who wasn't quite finished.

"I got one more point I'd like to make," he said. "When I talked to those kids on the roof, they told me they had seen a blue glow coming from the sniper's rifle."

"Starlight scope?" Fletcher asked.

"I don't think so. Hayes here tells me that's green. What the fuck glows blue?"

"Your ass in winter," Fletcher said.

"Your balls for the last ten years," Ryker said automatically.

"The color of your uniforms when I bust you to patrolman," Peterson said, stopping the conversation.

"Uh, could I say something?" Hayes asked. "When I was up at the Academy, I ran into one of my teachers, Lieutenant D'Angelo."

They all knew about D'Angelo. He was a gun freak who could tell you more than you wanted to know about every firearm from blunderbusses to Berettas.

"As you know, Starlight scopes are standard issue for ESU snipers. They have a five-power magnification and can be used in low light. Everything you see through them has a greenish glow, but is very clear. In rain or fog, the picture is blurred, due to light refraction from the moisture," Hayes said, realizing for the first time he had their attention. He liked the feeling of being in charge, but it made him nervous.

"You can't use a Starlight scope during daylight hours," Hayes continued. "Only at dusk or full night."

"But it's green, right?" Ryker asked.

"Yeah, and you could only see the glow if you were looking in a direct line of sight down the tube from the sniper's end, which is how these kids must have seen it. The other way is to look directly into the tube from the business end of the rifle—by that time the discovery won't do you much good, though."

The men laughed again. Fischetti spoke. "How far away can it be seen?"

Hayes scratched his head. "There's what's called a 'visual security distance.' That's the distance within which the green light can be seen, head-on. I don't remember the distance, though. We'll find out."

"One more thing: Does this scope actually take its power from starlight?" Fischetti asked.

"I'm not quite sure how it works exactly, but it does use the stars, moon and other light sources. It's electronic, and has a nickel/cadmium battery as its primary power source."

"What's the life expectancy on this battery? Can it be replaced?"

"About five hours continuous use. At approximately five minutes or less for each sniping, this gives him about sixty or so individual occurrences, assuming the battery was fully charged to begin with. I don't think we can wait him out on that basis. Also, I don't know if they can be replaced locally."

"That's real cute stuff, kid," Fletcher said. "But I thought the light was as blue as a frozen pussy."

"That's where it starts to get interesting," Hayes said. "Lieutenant D'Angelo told me that the Army has developed what they call the Mark V. Nobody knows much about it—it's that supersecret. But the word is that it casts a blue glow." Hayes added, "It's also about ten times as effective as the standard issue Starlight scope, uses much less power, is computerized, miniaturized. . . ."

"And most of all, dehumidified," Fletcher broke in. "Unlike this room."

Hayes looked hurt. "Well, the Mark V does almost everything except make the coffee in the morning."

"I assume you can't buy one," Peterson said.

"No, sir. If our man has one, it's got to be stolen from a military base or, more likely, an arsenal or testing center."

"Check it out," Peterson said. "All of you hit the street and track down Ryker's list of possibles."

"How about the derelict?" Fischetti asked taking notes.

"He'll be in here about six tonight for the other half of a twenty-dollar bill. Bums are hard to keep track of, but, meanwhile, let's separate the files with the Manhattan addresses," Ryker said.

As Ryker spoke, another detective entered the room. Seeing Peterson's back turned, he handed a message to Lieutenant Fischetti. Fischetti looked down at it and grinned. "These people are not wasting much time."

He read from the message. "Vero Beach, Florida Police Department reports that William Hart, a possible, is running a grocery store in town. Still there. Put an 'X' through that one, Hayes," Fischetti said. "These things will be pouring in hot and heavy the rest of the day."

Ryker broke in. "Hayes's had a rough night, so why doesn't he stay here and do the phone work?"

Fischetti spoke again. "Okay, good. Then you'll check out Manhattan?"

"Yeah. There looked like there were only three or four. I'll take care of them after the kids and Greek, if necessary, but I think I'll get a make from that Greek guy, if our boy's in these files," said Ryker.

"You want a partner?" Fischetti asked.

"I'll round up Bo Lindly," Ryker said. "If there's nothing else, thank you all for your time. Let's bring these outside and make copies."

A silence filled the room. One by one, the men began to look at Peterson, whose back was still to them.

Ryker broke the silence. "Maybe we're all wrong, boys. Maybe it wasn't a sniper. Maybe the Zoogs did it."

SIX

Outside the conference room, Fischetti turned to Ryker. "You shouldn't have said that, Joe."

"Couldn't help it, Lieutenant." Ryker walked toward the stairs. Hayes followed.

"What's this Zoog business?"

"Men from outer space," Ryker answered.

"Come on, Joe, damn it. Can't I get a straight answer for once?"

Ryker smiled. "No shit, from outer space." He paused and seemed to consider. "Okay, listen good, then forget it. Understand?"

"Sure."

"Well, we used to have a joke around here before Peterson. Deputy Inspector Connolly was just like Peterson, a political hack who thought he was Sherlock Holmes. Whenever we had a case that was a pisser—and I mean no leads at all—we used to say the Zoogs did it. Well, Connolly appreciated a little humor, but he started to use the phrase more and more. We all knew he was under a lot of strain. He had a rough assignment in a rough city—I don't have to tell you. Anyway, one day the Police Commissioner asked for a full report on a series of murders that we had nothing on."

Hayes could see the end of the story already.

Ryker continued. "So Connolly writes back that the Zoogs did it. He also blamed the Zoogs for a lot of other things around here. To make a long one short, the P.C. figured Connolly was ready for the rubber gun squad and had him carted off. He's in a funny farm out on Long Island now."

"What are you saying, Joe? You think Peterson's . . . ?"

"I didn't say a fucking thing," Ryker growled.

Downstairs, Ryker photocopied the print sheets. When he finished, he handed the originals to a patrolman and asked him to take them upstairs. He put his copies in a manila envelope and left the building.

On Sixth Street, he stopped at a pushcart and asked for a lemon ice. He was exhausted and hot. He sucked the ice, wishing he had a Benzedrine capsule—something to keep him up for a few more hours. He continued walking east until he came to the deserted tenement that had been the sniper's perch. The Crime Lab was about finished, he noticed, so he asked a lab man who was packing some gear in a police van if he had seen Detective Lindly.

"On the roof," the man said.

Ryker climbed the tenement stoop and passed through the foul-smelling foyer. He noticed that the walls, radiator, and banister were covered with dusting powder. An oddly shaped chalk line ran over the walls and down to the slimy floor, where the derelict had died on his knees. He hadn't noticed any of this in the dark last night.

Crime Lab must have had fun figuring out how to

outline that corpse. *It's not every day that a man dies on his knees with his dick in his hand,* Ryker thought as he slowly trudged up the stairs.

At the second landing, he stopped and leaned against the wall, his heart beating like a triphammer. His mouth was dry, and his skin felt cool and clammy.

After a few seconds, he pushed off from the wall and up the last flight. On the roof, Lindly sat on a low parapet that overlooked the street, writing in his notebook.

"Who in his goddamned right mind sits in this kind of sun doing his paperwork?"

Lindly looked up slowly, blinking the sun's glare out of his eyes. "Oh, what's up, J.R.? Make points with the Captain this morning?"

"Yeah, he promoted me to General."

Ryker moved over into the shadows and stood with his back against the brick wall. He removed his sunglasses. "Flip me a cigarette."

Lindly looked up from his notebook.

"Cigarette."

Lindly fingered a Marlboro out of his breast pocket and tossed it to Ryker. Ryker pulled off the filter, lit the cigarette, and sucked greedily. His hands shook, and his heart started thumping again. He smoked the cigarette until it burned his fingers, then let it drop.

Lindly began talking as he wrote. "I promised the wife and kids I'd take them to the beach for this summer's vacation. We're leaving in two days. I hate the damned beach, but I thought since I have to go, I might as well get a head start on my sun-conditioning. I burn pretty badly, you know, but I figured if I sit in the sun every chance I get . . ."

"We're working together now."

". . . I might be able to avoid . . ."

"This case will probably run through Labor Day."

". . . getting burned like last year."

"There won't be any more vacations until this is over."

"I would rather go to the mountains. The Catskills maybe, but we've rented a cottage already on the Jersey shore, and I . . ."

"You don't have to go along—you can't go."

Lindly finally acknowledged that he was listening. He looked desperate. "Joe, she'll kill me!"

"Stop being so goddamned pussy-whipped."

"Look, Joe, you don't understand family pressure. . . ." Lindly stopped abruptly. "Sorry."

Ryker ignored the remark. He tried to remember going away with Ellie, but he couldn't. Probably because they'd hardly left the city at all during their ten years of marriage. Hell, they hadn't even gone out much together. They were always too busy or too tired. It was fine for a while, when they were first together. You didn't need fancy entertainment when you were hot for each other—all you needed was a bed or a floor . . . or a roof. "Did you find anything new up here?" Ryker asked.

Lindly rose slowly and wiped his dripping face with a handkerchief. "Not really. Dusted the whole god-damned place. Hundreds of different prints. No shell casings. Nothing unusual that this guy might have dropped. How did you make out with that soda bottle?"

"Possible. Let's take a walk down to my favorite Greek restaurant. I'll tell you about it on the way."

"How about the lovebirds?"

"If there's any place a kid in New York isn't going to be on a day like this, it's in his apartment."

* * *

As the two cops walked south, Ryker kept an eye open for his witnesses as he filled Lindly in. They reached the Greek's without spotting any of them.

Lindly looked at the run-down, filthy structure. "Nice place."

"Coffee's terrific."

There was no air conditioning, and the temperature was about ten degrees higher inside than out. Ryker and Lindly looked around. The tables were fairly empty for lunch hour. The counter, however, was doing a brisk take-out business in cold drinks and ice cubes, for which the Greek was charging two bucks a bag. Ryker and the Greek spotted each other simultaneously.

"So?" Demetrius asked, coming around from behind the counter, wiping his hands on his grease-spattered apron.

"Now I know why they call it Greece," Lindly said, running a finger across the gray counter.

"So did he come back?" Ryker asked.

"I told you I would call if he did."

"Sure."

"This man—is it the sniper you look for?"

"Maybe."

The men stared at each other. *This bastard is taking another shot at the old eyeball-to-eyeball routine again,* Ryker thought, tiring of the game.

Ryker broke eye contact on purpose. The Greek's manliness was established this time, but only for a brief second. He followed Ryker's gaze across the room.

"Wife and kids?" Ryker asked, looking toward the counter. An olive-skinned woman with classically Greek features was pouring iced tea. *She must have been an attractive woman in her day,* Ryker thought.

Working beside her were a girl and boy in their teens. Their slim bodies moved quickly as they waited on the impatient customers.

"You didn't tell me you had help here, Demetrius."

The Greek looked back at Ryker, who was still looking at his family. He saw deep menace in the cop's eyes.

"They weren't here yesterday. They didn't see him."

"Of course they were here. They saw him."

"I saw him better," Demetrius said. "I looked right into his eyes, like I am looking into your eyes. They saw nothing."

Ryker put on his Porsche sunglasses. The Greek could see his own fear reflected back at him. The battle of wills, the battle of excessive pride, was over—the Greek had capitulated.

"So, what do you want?"

"Right in his eyes?"

"In his eyes—across the counter—nose to nose."

"Fine, let's look at some pictures."

"In the kitchen."

"After you."

Demetrius turned and moved his massive bulk around the counter and through a swinging door. He said something in Greek as he passed his wife. Ryker and Lindly followed.

If the diner was hot, the small, fetid kitchen was hell. Greasy cloying odors hung in the steamy air. Lindly thought he would faint or puke, probably both.

"Table," Ryker said.

The Greek motioned to a bloody butcher block table in the middle of the small room. The two men faced off on either side of it. Lindly moved toward the back door for some air. Ryker removed the print sheets from the manila envelope and spread them on the table. He began to turn through them without any preliminaries. The Greek put his big hands on the bloody table and stared down as the pictures flipped by. Ryker had started off with the criminal files. As he reached the first military file, he asked, "Him?"

"No."

"Him?"

"No."

"Him?"

"No."

The drill went on until the questions and answers came to sound like a medieval chant. Drops of sweat splashed on the flipping pages.

"Him?"

"No."

"Him?"

Silence.

The Greek lifted his hand and put a big finger, bloody from the butcher block, on the page. "Him."

Lindly moved over from where he was breathing the stink from the back-alley garbage pails. Ryker turned the page around and looked at the picture. The Greek's big finger left a bloody smudge over the face of Henry Cyrus.

The two cops stared at the picture for a long moment. Ryker pulled a crumpled twenty-dollar bill from his pocket and threw it on the table. The big Greek pushed the bill back across the bloody surface. He turned to Lindly. "Your friend looks for a killer, but he smells of death himself."

The Greek turned and walked out slowly through the swinging door. Ryker and Lindly left through the back.

The alley seemed cooler, if nothing else, and the

men lingered a moment. Ryker took another cigarette from Lindly and removed his sunglasses.

"I guess he smelled the burnt hair and flesh. It sort of clings to the clothes, you know."

Ryker looked up. "Maybe."

"Why don't you go home and get cleaned up a bit? I'll hustle up those kids and bring them down to the station."

"You don't even know what they look like."

"They all look alike, anyway. I'll just hustle up the first Spanish kid I see with jism on his cock and haul him in."

"They're all about fourteen and the guys all have jism on their cocks. Instead of you checking out dicks for recent signs of sexual intercourse the rest of the afternoon, I'll look. Let's eat."

As they made their way through the rubble- and garbage-strewn alley, a tremendous rat glared at them from an overturned garbage pail. It could have easily eaten a medium-sized dog.

Out on the sun-scorched street, the men turned into a nondescript restaurant and sat down in a booth. Ryker smoked another of Lindly's cigarettes, then he placed a file on the table: "Cyrus, Henry—RA 1239744—U.S. Army, Infantry—Private First Class—U.S. citizen—born Coffeyville, Kansas, 17 April '53—released from active duty, 8 May '75—last duty, Fort Jackson, South Carolina—date of entry into service, 16 January '73—character of service, honorable—Military Occupation Specialty, 11B10, small arms, infantry—Home of Record, 143 Harrow Street, Coffeyville, Kansas—decorations: National Defense Service Medal, Vietnam Service Medal, Combat Infantryman Badge, Vietnam Campaign Medal, Purple Heart—remarks: U.S. Army Hospital,

Japan; Oakland, California, May '74 to May '75. VA Hospital, Oakland, California, May '75 to the present."

"What is he, a cripple?" Lindly asked. "All this time in a VA hospital?"

"He's a cripple, all right, but it's his brain that's fucked up, according to this. He's in the psycho ward of that hospital," Ryker said.

"Not anymore, apparently," Lindly said. "Can we check it right now?"

"Yeah," Ryker said, and went to call Hayes. When he finished, he went back to join Lindly.

"If he's busted out, you think he's the guy?" Lindly asked, flipping through the report.

"Sure, he was an LRRP," Ryker said. "Long-range reconnaissance patrol. Those were tough-assed mothers who out-gooked the gooks, living off the land, eating snakes, and blowing away NVA officers right in their home bases."

A waitress approached cautiously. She stared intently at her pad. "Order?"

"Beer in a bottle, no glass, please," Lindly said.

"Two, no—three hamburgers, bottle of beer," Ryker said.

"No hamburgers, sir."

"What?"

"No beef."

Ryker eyed the sari-clad waitress for the first time. "Oh, Christ, a fucking Indian restaurant. Just beer, then."

"No beer, sir. No license."

"Coffee?"

"Yes, sir."

"Make it two," Lindly said.

Ryker looked around the battered restaurant. At

least it was air-conditioned, or more precisely, almost air-conditioned. One of the units was broken, and an old, clanking machine was trying to do the work of two. Ryker could sympathize.

The phone on the wall rang, and Ryker answered it before it shrilled a second time.

"Let's go," he said to Lindly when he had hung up. "I think we got our man. He disappeared from the Oakland VA hospital six months ago."

"What's he doing here?" Lindly asked, standing up. "Why isn't he in Coffeeburg or wherever?"

"All the psychos wind up here. This is psycho mecca," Ryker said, throwing a dollar down on the table.

Out on the street, Ryker walked past the waiting customers at a pushcart and bought four hot dogs, two for Lindly. The people in line didn't say a word about being aced out by the smelly, disheveled Ryker. They figured he either had the biggest pair of balls in town or was a dangerous nut job. Either way, they didn't want to mess with him.

"You know, Joe," Lindly said while munching on a hot dog, "you're looking less and less like a respectable member of the community."

Ryker belched.

"Furthermore, you'd function better with some sleep and a clean change of clothing," he continued, trying to sound helpful and reasonable.

"Did I ever tell you to go fuck off?"

"Lots of times."

"Give me a cigarette—I'll find the kids, then I'm going to hit the sack. I'll be back at the station at six to grill the bum, if he shows. You meet me there."

"Okay."

"Go back to the station house now and fill them in.

See if Peterson wants to call off the nationwide based on this make. Call the Coffeyville police. If they haven't checked Cyrus yet . . ." Ryker paused.

"Yeah?"

"Tell them to hold off. If somebody he knows still lives there, the cops will spook them. Tell them to make discreet inquiries."

"Right. Discreet."

"Call Army Personnel at Saint Louis and get his complete two-o-one file, including medical."

"Right."

Ryker pulled the files from Lindly's hand, unbuttoned his shirt, and slid the envelope inside. He thought he had his man and decided not to follow up on the other Manhattan addresses. What he wanted was an identification from the kids and the derelict, so he decided to look for them and get it over with as quickly as possible—he felt sure that nightfall would bring another sniping.

Street people and kids were not that difficult to find, if you knew where to look for them. Ryker began with the East River. Kids were sometimes crazy enough to swim in that open polluted sewer when it got hot enough. He checked the area around the projects where an old rotting raft made it the favorite swimming spot for miles. Nobody was crazy enough for swimming today, though.

From there, he walked back west, past the public school. Kids hung around schools even in the summer, whether there was a playground attached or not. They used the walls and steps for handball, stoopball, sitting, and leaning, as well as smoking, drinking, and injecting drugs. But he had no luck. He turned back toward the water and checked the small unnamed park attached to the Lillian Wald Houses. No bum. No Romeo or Juliet.

The park contained a huge, graffiti-encrusted bandshell and some scanty vegetation. Looking around, Ryker saw a line of bushes moving furiously. There was no wind to cause them to stir with such vigor, so Ryker walked over. "What's going on in there?" he bellowed.

"Just necking," came a voice.

"Put your neck back in your pants and get the hell out here."

A young Spanish boy rose unsteadily from the bushes, fixing his pants. It wasn't the right one, but Ryker figured he'd have a go at him anyway.

"Your girlfriend shy?"

The kid shrugged.

"You kids do anything except fuck all day?"

The kid shrugged again.

"Do you know Hector Lopez and Maria Ferrara?"

A third shrug.

"You're a fucking fountain of information, aren't you?" Ryker said. "Maybe your girlfriend's a little more talkative." He called out, "Yo, sweetheart, get your pretty ass out here."

The bushes rustled, and Ryker, knowing she was trying to get away, hurdled the bushes and landed atop the prone figure on the other side. His foot sank into the soft flesh of the buttocks. He lost his balance and fell. The figure whimpered. Turning around on his hands and knees, Ryker looked into the eyes of a terrified boy, about twelve years old.

"Well, well," Ryker said, standing. "Get up, Juanita. I'm looking for Hector Lopez and Maria Ferrara. And you'd better know where they are."

The boy spoke little English, and Ryker even less

Spanish, but the boy managed to convey to Ryker that there was a small club room in the basement of a building on East Second Street. They might be there.

The boy stood with his head bowed after he finished speaking. Ryker's hand shot out and grabbed the boy's cheek under his left eye. He pinched and twisted the maxillary nerve, which caused the boy a tremendous amount of pain. The Hispanic boy went white beneath his dusky skin.

"A piece of fatherly advice, Juanita. Get yourself a good piece of pussy and you unload this *maricón*, here," he said, nodding toward the older boy. *"Sabe?"*

"Sí! Sí!" the boy screamed, tearing himself from Ryker's grasp. He and his boyfriend ran off, hand in hand.

Ryker sighed and walked south to Second Street. He was angry for not thinking of the basement himself. He could always grab them in their apartments that night, but he had a feeling that the sniper would add another notch to his gun after the sun went down. The sooner he could get Peterson to put out an all points for Henry Cyrus, the sooner he might be spotted on the street by a passing patrol car.

Ryker had felt he was racing against time ever since he stood on the shattered FDR Drive seventeen hours earlier. He wondered what was going on inside the sniper's head right now. Was he sleeping—resting for tonight's work? Had Ryker passed right by the killer's lair during his wanderings through these decaying neighborhoods? Where was his hide-out? A respectable apartment? A deserted tenement? An unused dock? A tree in a park? Every time Ryker saw a blond man, which was rare in this neighborhood, he quickened his pace until he came abreast of him. Every lounging bum caught his eye, and he looked twice at every Hispanic boy and girl. He had second thoughts about the derelict. What if he didn't show tonight?

Ryker glanced at his watch. Two-fifteen. At a small candy store, he bought a pack of cigars. Standing at the head of East Second Street, he looked down the line of stoops that protruded from the tenements. These stoops were usually a place for sitting and socializing in the slum neighborhoods, but the intense heat rising from the stone had driven the kids to the open fire hydrant at the end of the block. The adults had retreated with their infants to the few scattered parks and air-conditioned movie theaters uptown, where they sat all day watching insipid love stories or unintelligible documentaries.

Ryker moved quickly toward a building on East Second Street. The outer door opened, but the inner—a steel one—was locked.

Ryker retreated and tried the building next door. It was open, but the door at the back of the foyer, which led to a small backyard, was nailed shut. Ryker cursed silently and began the long trek up the stairs to the roof. On the roof, he stared at the insurmountable wall of the next building. Next, he leaned over the edge of the back parapet. A rusting fire escape began one floor below. Without stopping to think about it, Ryker vaulted the parapet and dropped. As his weight crashed onto the unsteady structure, he could hear the creaking and groaning of old metal. Rusted welds snapped, and toggle bolts pulled loose from decayed mortar. He scrambled down the ladders and past the landings. At the last landing he discovered that the ladder to the ground was missing. He paused and lit a cigar. After a few minutes, he urinated in a long arch to the ground below. Looking down at his rust-streaked suit, he wondered how Lindly always looked so dapper. If he stood absolutely motionless, he noticed, the fire escape wouldn't make those disturbing creaks and groans.

Ten feet below him was a jungle of late August weed growth. Ragweeds and milkweeds five feet tall choked the small yards around him. Leaning fences of every type of construction ran between the yards. Another hiding place for a killer, Ryker realized. Next door, he could just see the back entrance to the cellar, which was his goal.

Incredibly, here and there, he could make out disused outhouses. Many of these buildings had been built in the last century, and the central plumbing was added later by reluctant landlords as a small concession to the twentieth century. "No one bothered to cart away the old shithouses," Ryker said aloud.

Through the weeds below, he could see mounds of garbage and rusting metal interspersed with glittering glass. Clenching the cigar between his teeth, he leaped. He landed heavily, though feet first, and sunk into tangled bedsprings. The wires tore into his ankles as he pitched forward. He took the brunt of the fall with his outspread arms, pitching onto a mound of shattered glass. As he got slowly to his feet, he noticed a large bloodstain spreading on the left sleeve of his tan jacket. He was spotted with garbage and dog feces. As he checked for his guns, he made a mental note to see about a tetanus shot.

A quick hurdle put him over the adjoining fence. He descended the dank outside staircase, spit out his cigar and slid quietly through the basement door.

Inside, he crouched and blinked until he could see in the semidarkness. He rubbed his bleeding ankles as he waited. On the opposite end of the basement was a wooden wall which must have once been the coal bin. Behind it, he heard Salsa music and adolescent laughter. Ryker moved toward the small door in the wall.

He could smell marijuana. Gently, he tried the latch. The door was locked from the inside. Splintering doors gave him a strange pleasure that he couldn't quite put into words. Everyone on the other side was always so surprised. He smiled as he stepped back. In three long strides his shoulder hit the door; his hurtling bulk made matchwood of the rotted boards.

Instant pandemonium broke loose inside the small room as pieces of the door flew in all directions. Girls screamed, and the boys went for their knives. The boom box fell over, and the tape stopped. An expectant silence filled the small enclosure. Ryker stood in the doorway and looked around. The air was thick with incense and marijuana smoke.

"Pardon me, is this where the Four-H Club meets?"

"Who are you, man?"

"Police."

The wolf-faced boy who had spoken looked Ryker up and down. "Bullshit."

"He *is* the police, Orlando."

Ryker recognized the young feminine voice.

"Ferrara, Lopez—outside," he ordered.

Orlando spoke. "Says who, man?"

"Says Mr. Ruger, asshole." Ryker slowly drew the big .357 Magnum from his shoulder holster and pulled back the heavy hammer. The two loud clicks sounded like a crypt door closing in the eerie stillness of the room.

"Okay, man. Okay."

The boy and girl slid past the cop and stood outside.

"All knives on the floor, kiddies." Ryker could hear at least ten distinct sounds of metal against the concrete. He still could not make out the number of people in the room.

"All, I said," he chanced.

Two more knives hit the floor.

"All right, all the crack, all the nose candy, all the reefer in one bag. Got it?"

They scurried around, collecting the loot. Ryker caught the brown bag as it sailed toward him.

"Everybody—outside!" Ryker backed out first and let thirteen kids slide by.

"Stand in the light—by the door—quickly."

Ryker holstered his gun and surveyed the group before him. It occurred to him that he had spent the last twenty-four hours or so breaking up other people's good times.

"Okay, children—now there's a bum who hangs out around here." Ryker described the derelict down to the torn twenty dollar bill in his pocket. "His name is Bob Reid. *Saben?*" He continued, "The first one to bring him here gets this shit back." He held up the bag.

There was an audible sigh of relief from the assemblage in front of him. No bust. A weird guy for a policeman, but so what? All Anglos were a little weird.

"Half hour," Ryker said, "Ferrara, Lopez, you stay here. You too, *lobo,*" he called at their retreating backs, using the Spanish word for wolf. The wolf-faced boy, Orlando, knew that Ryker meant him. He didn't like it at all. *Some cops let you mouth off to 'em, some take it personal,* he thought. *This cop was no* maricón.

Orlando turned and caught Ryker's fist square on his long, sloping jaw. He toppled like a cut tree. The other kids never looked back.

Maria Ferrara and Hector Lopez were reliving a little bit of last night's terror. Ryker walked over to them, thrust his hand into his shirt, and pulled out the manila folder. "Are you two high?"

"No."

He took the girl by the arm and looked into her eyes.

There was no dilation of the pupils. Ryker sat on the bottom step of the outside stairs and pulled the girl down with him. Sunlight poured down on their backs.

"Into the other room, Lopez."

Ryker started going through the pictures. The girl looked uncomfortable. Ryker realized that he stunk. "Once you get past the dog shit and garbage, I'm really quite a nice guy, you know."

"Huh?"

"Concentrate on the pictures."

The girl looked at the flipping pages for a few minutes. She wanted to please this terrifying man at any cost but, finally, she began to sob. "We only saw his back—it was dark!"

"You saw his profile as he ran down the stairs. You saw him from the top as he walked down the street."

"It was dark," she sobbed.

Ryker knew she was right. He thought, at least twenty feet distance—back view, fleeing profile, dusk to dark—it would never stand up even if she could pick him.

Unlike police mug shots, the Army files included only a full-face picture. Ryker decided to go ahead anyway. When he came to Henry Cyrus's picture, the girl leaned forward.

"Him?"

"No."

Cyrus's file was well-creased and bore a bloody fingerprint. That's what made her look, he realized. Ryker grasped the girl's arm. "That's him," he said angrily. "That's him!"

"Okay, okay."

Disgusted, Ryker stood up. "Lopez!" On the floor, Orlando stirred briefly, then lapsed back into unconsciousness. Hector Lopez came quickly from the room. Ryker sent the girl back in and began again.

The boy also looked twice at Cyrus's manhandled file, but no luck.

Ryker heard a noise behind him and whirled around. Coming down the stairs was a Spanish girl. She was furiously pulling someone by the arm. Ryker looked up the stairwell. At the end of the girl's arm was the old derelict, Bob Reid.

He saw Ryker and began complaining. "I was coming, for Christ's sake! You said six o'clock, for Christ's sake. Sweet Jesus, girlie, leggo my arm!" The bum was very drunk.

Ryker smiled, "I was afraid you might forget me, Grandpa. Let's see that half a twenty."

The bum stammered, "I—uh—got rolled . . . right after you left. Never a cop around when you need one."

"Brought it to the bank for a ten, did you, old timer?"

"Needed a drink," the drunk admitted sheepishly. "But hell, I woulda showed up at six for the other half."

"Maybe." Ryker was suddenly glad that he had trusted his instinct and had the bum pulled in. He knew that a vagrant like this could disappear forever into the slums of the city.

The girl who had brought him in had noticed the still body on the floor. Orlando was fully conscious now but had decided to stay put. A trickle of blood ran across the concrete from under his mouth. His eyes were open and the girl thought he was dead. She became frightened. The derelict saw the same thing and began to shake.

Ryker tossed the bag of drugs into the girl's wide-eyed face. She barely flinched. Ryker grabbed the old man by the arm and led him up the stairs. He entered the foyer from the open rear door, and passed through the front door and down the stoop.

On the street, the derelict turned to him. "Why did you kill that guy?"

"He had trouble identifying a picture."

At the station house, Ryker prodded the old man across the lobby. The big clock over the desk read 4:05 P.M. The day-shift desk sergeant was just leaving. He looked at Ryker and shook his head. *This man would be joining Inspector Connolly shortly,* he thought, *at the funny farm.*

As Ryker approached the staircase, a passing patrolman grabbed his arm. "Where you two foxy grandpas going?"

Ryker removed his sunglasses. The eyes were rheumy and swollen, but the patrolman knew them. He touched the bill of his cap, mumbled something and moved off.

Ryker half-dragged the old derelict up the stairs to the squad room. Ryker's bedraggled appearance caused everyone to look up. He dropped the bum into a chair and sat himself down at the head of the long table in the middle of the room. Fischetti waved everyone over.

"You all right?"

"Yeah."

"Is that our witness?"

"That's him."

"The kids?"

"They couldn't make him. I'll drag them in one day to make a statement, though."

"Shit—they were our only real witnesses."

"I know. Where's Peterson?"

"Gone. Right after you left this morning. Lindly

filled us in on the Greek, then he went home, too. Tired, he said."

"That's nice. How are you making out here?"

"Routine. Almost every possible is accounted for so far. The Coffeyville Police said Henry Cyrus hasn't been spotted since he split the psycho ward. The only family he has is an unmarried sister with a kid. She hasn't heard from him in years, she says."

"How about his Army file from Saint Louis?"

"It's on the way. The FBI man is bringing it, personally."

"Let's put out an all points for this guy, Lieutenant."

"Let's get a better make from him, first," Fischetti said, motioning toward the drunk.

"I'd go on the Greek's make. This old fart won't be sober for hours."

Fischetti was in a quandary. He cursed Peterson for leaving. "I don't want to put everyone in a tizzy yet. How much has this guy had?"

Ryker looked toward the drunk. "At least ten dollars' worth. He brought my half a twenty to a bank," he said.

Fischetti walked over to the derelict, whose head was lolling from side to side. He yanked his head up by his greasy hair. "Smells like whiskey."

"He's drunker now than when I collared him. Let's puke him."

"We'll take care of it. Get some rest and see to that arm. See you in the morning," Fischetti said.

"Shit, I'm dressed for a puking. Hayes, you ever straighten a drunk?"

Hayes had been wondering when his partner was going to acknowledge him. "No, not really."

"Come on, give us a hand," he said to Detective John Littel.

The three men carried the drunk into the men's room. Hayes got the disagreeable job of stripping the incredibly filthy derelict. Fischetti came in with a box of salt and a glass, and the men propped the naked bum in front of the toilet bowl. Ryker held Reid's nose, and Littel pried his mouth open.

Then Hayes poured two glasses of warm salt water down his throat. The drunk wiggled and gurgled. He became so frightened that he urinated on Littel's shoes.

"This fuck doesn't want to blow all that good Panther Piss," Littel said, wiping his shoes on the drunk's back.

Ryker became impatient. He knelt down and delivered a medium force blow to the drunk's abdomen.

"Stand back!"

The old man vomited copiously in and around the bowl. The white porcelain was splotched with every color of the rainbow.

"We should have taken him to the drunk tank for this," Littel grimaced.

"It's more fun here," Ryker said.

They repeated the salt water treatment until the derelict began bringing up bile and acid.

"Clean as a hound's tooth," Littel said.

The derelict looked pale; Hayes looked worse. Ryker dragged the bum to the middle of the floor. Fischetti took a bucket from the janitor's closet and poured disinfectant in it. Littel filled it with hot water. Ryker put his hands over the old man's face.

"Bombs away, John. Don't get any on me."

"You could use it more," Littel said as he poured the mixture over the naked figure.

Littel refilled the bucket with cold water and splashed it down the length of the inert figure. The old man yelped.

"That's got it. A few more buckets full."

Finally, Ryker propped the drunk against the wall. He was shivering and pale, and began to turn blue. Fischetti left and came back with a container of cream from the coffee table. Ryker poured it down Reid's throat. He drooled half of it down his chin. Littel hit him in the face with another bucket of cold water.

"That's enough," Ryker said. He was getting splashed, too.

They dragged the old man, still naked, into the squad room and sat him in a chair. He started to shake uncontrollably.

"Coffee," Ryker said. "Peterson's," he added as an afterthought.

Hayes came back with a mug of coffee from Peterson's office.

"The way he makes this stuff, it would raise the dead," he said as he poured the sludge into the old man's mouth. As though a miracle were taking place, Reid opened his eyes and asked for another cup. Three cups later, he sat upright. He looked across the room at a wall clock. "Five-fifteen. I'm early."

The men laughed.

Ryker started to peel his own jacket off to put over the old man's shoulders, but the coagulated blood on his arm glued the jacket to his skin. Fischetti gave it a yank and ripped it loose. He dropped it over the shivering bum's shoulders.

"Let him get his head together," Ryker said. He walked to the men's room and washed. Later, they all sat around the table as the old man, sober now, looked through the pictures. Without hesitation, he fingered Henry Cyrus.

Fischetti stood. "Let's get an all points out. We have about two hours until dark." He looked at the derelict. "We'll lock him up in protective custody."

The old man began to complain. Everyone ignored him.

"We have to be careful of those assholes from the Civil Liberties Union," Ryker said. "You remember what happened last time when we forgot somebody in the drunk tank."

Fischetti looked concerned. "We'll fix it up. We'll get his written permission." He turned to the old man. "Right, Pops?"

Ryker grabbed his jacket and headed toward the stairs. As he reached them, he turned around. "Hayes?"

"Yeah?"

"Seven in the morning. Here."

"Right."

Fischetti called, "Joe, if he shoots again tonight, do you want us to call you?"

"No."

Ryker walked in a trance back to his apartment. The first phase of the case was over. His mind was blank. His arm throbbed. Every nerve and fiber of his body ached for rest. In his apartment, he left a trail of clothing between his door and the bedroom. Standing naked in the bathroom, he ran the water for a hot shower. He looked in the steamy mirror, then looked away quickly. He wasn't a pretty sight.

When he stepped out of the shower, he felt relaxed and calm for the first time in days, Kicking the dirty clothes out of the way, he went to his bedroom and opened his closet door. Inside were three identical tan summer suits; three cheap, white short-sleeve shirts; and three blue-and-maroon striped ties—all knotted and ready to be slipped around his neck.

I'll have to go to the cleaners soon, he thought, shutting the door. The fat Chink that ran the place shuddered every time Ryker came in with his dirty laundry. He wasn't used to handling blood, pus, shit, piss, vomit, and mung. He was also unnerved by Ryker's wardrobe. Six identical summer suits, six identical winter suits, six short-sleeve shirts, six long-sleeve shirts, all white, and six identical ties, for winter or summer.

Ryker hated shopping almost as much as he hated the scumbags in the street.

That was the one good thing about being married, he thought, setting the alarm on his clock radio. Ellie bought all his clothes for him. She also used to . . .

But he was asleep before he could even think about her warm, red mouth.

SEVEN

A light rain began falling at six P.M. The rain turned to steamy mist as the water absorbed the tremendous quantities of heat stored in Manhattan's stone, concrete, and tar. Lieutenant Fischetti looked out the second story window of the station house. He turned slowly to Hayes. "Didn't you say that the fog and such makes that scope inoperative?"

"More or less inoperative, I guess. Reduces the range. I don't know about this new scope, though, so who knows what he can do?"

"He's still in business all right. I'd bet on it."

The heavy clouds brought an early dusk to the city; rush hour traffic was snarled on the streets below. Fischetti snapped on additional lights. They cast a sickly yellow glare over the almost deserted squad room. By now, every patrol car in New York City had or was getting Henry Cyrus's picture. Every Anti-Crime Squad plainclothes man had, or was getting, the picture also.

Hayes called his wife and explained why he

wouldn't be home again that evening. He and Fischetti went to a neighborhood bar for dinner. They had both decided to stick around until something happened.

Less than four blocks from where Hayes and Fischetti were eating, a man walked slowly north along Avenue A. If he had any idea that he might be the subject of a massive police search, he didn't seem to care. In actuality, there was no reason why he should care. Last night's medium-length blond hair was now long and black. He carried the classic gun transporter—a long, black, bass violin case. Cyrus glanced down at the black case and smiled. The absolute beauty of a military weapon was the ease with which it could be broken down into its main components without the use of tools. A sharp yank on the trigger guard and the weapon came apart: firing mechanism, barrel and receiver group, stock group. Less than five seconds to disassemble. Less than ten seconds to reassemble. The whole process could be done in pitch darkness. It would be done that way tonight.

The rain began to let up. Henry Cyrus shifted the case to his other hand. He did not want anyone to notice that the case was much heavier than a bass violin should have been. The total weight, including the Starlight scope, came to just under twenty-five pounds. The disassembled length of thirty-one inches fit snugly into the case.

Cyrus could have put his mind at ease about attracting attention. New Yorkers rarely noticed anything unusual: partly because there was little that they considered unusual, and partly because the city was a nut magnet. Cyrus could have walked down the street in a Viking outfit (there was somebody on West

Fifty-fourth Street that did just that every day), and he would have hardly attracted a glance. If he was concerned about the police being suspicious of the violin case, he needn't have been. It was a far more common sight in New York than he supposed. The East Village was the home of hundreds of musicians. In addition, the whole area was dotted with local repertory groups and hole-in-the-wall theaters. To a cop, Cyrus might be just another slightly seedy musician returning from an audition or going to work.

Cooper Union on Seventh Street is one of the few bright spots in the generally dark and dreary landscape of the East Village. It lies on the border of the West Village and is a kind of no-man's land between East and West: a buffer zone; a New York City Balkans.

Cyrus looked around, choosing a perch, when a police car cruised slowly by and stopped opposite him across the street. He froze. The two young cops in the car considered him a moment. Cyrus began walking again. He nervously fingered an M-26 fragmentation grenade in the oversized pocket of his bush jacket. He heard the words "bush jackets" from the open squad car window. The pull ring of the grenade was tied to his belt by a nylon string which ran through his pocket. He gave the grenade a small yank. The tug pulled the safety pin from the grenade. Only Cyrus's sweating fingers held the safety lever in place.

The police car kept abreast of the walking figure. Cyrus slowly drew the live grenade from his pocket. The young cops, though, had decided he wasn't their man, and drove off. Cyrus noticed that his mouth had become dry and his heart was beating rapidly. "Just like the old days," he breathed with a smile. Before the hospital, before . . .

Cyrus walked west, crossing Lafayette Street,

Fourth Avenue, Broadway and University Place, then south along University to Washington Square Park. He passed the NYU dorms, alive with kids too hot and horny to sleep, and entered the madness of the park.

Two mimes were taking turns holding a flashlight on each other while they practiced their "craft," street musicians were playing, drug dealers and muggers weren't. Everybody was wrecked on something.

On the north side of the park, Cyrus found a stand of bedraggled forsythia bushes and knelt down in the wet grass. He set the violin case down and carefully replaced the safety pin in the grenade without removing it from his pocket. His fingers trembled around the safety lever.

"Have to get rid of the old bush jacket," he said sadly. He looked slowly down at the black case at his feet. Thoughts were forming in his disturbed brain. "They're on to us, Mikey. Somehow they got on to us, old buddy." He looked a little unhappy for a moment, then brightened. "We'll show them we can do any damn thing we take a mind to doin' and nobody's gonna stop us. We're tired of gettin' pushed around, ain't we, old buddy?"

It was getting darker. Cyrus got to his feet and snatched up the case. He walked a few yards and stopped. A good-sized tree seemed to be the perfect perch. He climbed the tree easily and settled in its leafy branches.

He awoke about midnight and sat listening to the night creatures in the park. They were still partying, though they were more subdued than before. When he was satisfied that he was alone, he grabbed a handful of large wet linden leaves and rubbed the sleep from his face. The rain had turned to light drizzle, but that didn't matter with a Mark V scope. In the distance, he could hear the muffled sound of traffic on University Place. Quickly, he unpacked the rifle, assembled it, and mounted the scope. He kicked the violin case out of the tree to give himself more room.

He played with the knobs and dials on the scope, adjusting it, tuning it. The moisture in the air was causing light to refract, but the microchip was adjusting nicely. He waited and fidgeted, and sighted for twenty minutes.

A young couple walked north on LaGuardia Place. They had just seen a dozen novice comedians at the Village Gate and were in high spirits. At the entrance to the park, they hesitated. The girl lived in the dorms on University Place, but she was afraid of the park at night. The young man thought she was being silly. After all, she had him to protect her. He laughed at her apprehension and pulled her arm toward the dimly-lit park.

"I'm only thinking of you," he said. "Wouldn't want you raped unless I had my camera along."

She giggled. "There're so many queers around here—*you'd* probably be the one to get raped."

She twirled her umbrella playfully as they began the walk toward the park.

In the tree, five hundred yards away, the killer watched the brief exchange through his scope. When he realized that the couple was coming toward him, he smiled. A few targets had passed already, but he dismissed them all. He was waiting for a particular quarry. As the girl moved closer he could make out the long, light blue hair streaming over her light blue raincoat. Blond hair, tan coat. He could translate shades of blue into their true colors with some degree of accuracy.

Two hundred and fifty yards. Young. Pretty. Too easy. A lot of light. Don't even need the scope.

A small breeze shook Cyrus's perch. He cursed softly. This would be an easy shot except for the unsteady limb. A target that moved from left to right or right to left was a little more difficult. A target moving directly away or directly forward did not appear to move at all. It loomed larger or smaller in the scope as it decreased or increased its distance. Generally, it could be treated as a stationary target. The girl did not appear to move in the scope. She simply grew larger.

Two hundred yards.

Joe Ryker was dreaming about his ex-wife; Bo Lindly was in his raised-ranch on Long Island, dreaming about sex on a New York rooftop; Captain Peterson was at a dinner with police and City Hall officials; Fischetti and Hayes were into their third hour of gin rummy in the precinct conference room. Other detectives were on- or off-duty, in the squad room, home or on the street.

Fischetti and Hayes got up and stretched. The thermometer still hung around eighty-five degrees in spite of the rain. The humidity was ninety-five percent. Hayes spoke. "I guess I'll be getting back to my hotel room. Too late to go home. Again."

"Right. I think this weather kept him quiet tonight."

"Hell, he may be clean across the country by now."

Fischetti looked thoughtful. "I don't think so. I know his type. He's from out of town. Came to New York like a lot of other people that come here—to make his mark. We attract them all."

"Including me and Joe Ryker."

"How are you getting along with him?" Fischetti asked.

"Okay, I guess. He's not exactly talkative, you know?"

"Except when he should keep his mouth shut. Like this morning with Peterson."

"He'll never be a captain, I guess," Hayes said.

"He'll be lucky to stay a sergeant," Fischetti said, wiping the sweat from his face with a hairy arm. Fischetti was the hairiest guy Hayes had ever seen. The lieutenant had a pelt of body hair, practically no forehead—just bushy eyebrows meeting a low scalp line; hair covered his hands, cascaded out of his nostrils and plugged up his ears; his beard laughed at razors. *It must be like wearing a hair shirt in this weather,* Hayes decided, nodding in agreement.

"But I don't suppose Ryker *wants* to be anything other than he is," Fischetti continued. "He's as happy as he ever gets when he's working."

"And he's good, too, I guess," Hayes said, edging toward the door. He'd rather hit the rack than bullshit all night with the lieutenant.

"You don't know how good, kid," Fischetti said. "So good the brass hasn't nailed him to the wall yet. Though they've tried hard enough. So good, he's still alive."

"Well."

"So good . . . aw, shit. You gotta admire a man like that," Fischetti said.

"Long's you don't have to be like him, I guess," Hayes said. Conversations about people who weren't around to defend themselves made Hayes uncomfortable, but he hoped to exhaust Fischetti's interest in Ryker quickly and get the hell out of the station house for the night, so he continued. "I don't mean how rough he is on the street, either. I know enough to know there are two sets of rules. One for assholes like

Peterson, the A.C.L.U., and the Harvard law professors, and one for the scumbags."

Fischetti nodded.

"I mean he's totally out of touch with what's going on in the world. He doesn't listen to music, he doesn't read books, he doesn't even watch TV, except for the news. He's never heard of any movie stars or politicians or astronauts or anything else. He just lives his current case. It's got to be the most boring life in the world," Hayes finished up.

"Maybe he collects stamps," Fischetti said.

"Yeah, so he can stick 'em on my ass and mail me back to Queens," Hayes said. "Sometimes I think he likes me; other times, I'm afraid he'll shoot me."

"He's a mystery, all right," Fischetti said.

"Not one I'd like to solve, particularly," Hayes said, grabbing his damp, stained jacket from the table and disappearing through the door.

Henry Cyrus was wet, tired, and uncomfortable, but he was used to that. He knew it was all worth it.

Two hundred yards.

The girl turned slightly to say something to her boyfriend. Cyrus placed the crosshairs in the middle of her profiled breast and squeezed the trigger. The tree shook with the silent report of the gun. Cyrus was showered with loosened raindrops.

The girl spun around as though she were doing a pirouette. The boy thought she was being playful and grabbed for her. She collapsed into the wet gutter without a sound. Her large polka-dotted umbrella covered her body. The young man pulled the umbrella away. The front of the girl's raincoat was red with blood. She was moaning softly, but when she raised her head and saw the blood, she screamed long and loud. In mid-scream, her body gave an involuntary jerk. Her raised kneecap was suddenly a mass of bone, blood, and frayed muscle. Another small jerk and her shoe and part of her left foot flew off. It seemed to the boy that his girlfriend, for some reason that he couldn't explain, was coming apart in front of his eyes. Another jerk and the moaning body lay still.

The boy screamed.

EIGHT

At two-fifteen A.M., Peterson called the small meeting to order in the conference room. He had been passed a note at the Oak Bar in the Plaza Hotel. The earlier dinner party had adjourned there, and Peterson was still a little drunk. He was a surly, rather than a happy, drunk, and he showed it. Also sitting around the long table was Lieutenant Fischetti, who had reached his home on Long Island just in time to turn around again; Arthur Hayes, who was in the process of fucking his blond whore when he received a phone call; and Louis Fernandez, who was the first detective on the scene. Ryker had been called at Peterson's insistence, but did not answer the phone. Nobody volunteered to go wake him at his apartment. At the far end of the table was John Avery, from the Federal Bureau of Investigation, just in from Washington, D.C.

Peterson spoke. "We all pretty well know what happened from our pre-meeting chatter, but give it to us again, Fernandez. Briefly."

The fat, good-natured detective stood. "This couple is walking along LaGuardia Place," he began from notes. "Toward the park, they walk." He looked up. "Remember, now, the only witness is the boyfriend, and he's pretty shook up." He told the story briefly and concluded. "So the last round passed through the girl's buttocks. She was taken to Bellevue Hospital. She died—about thirty minutes ago. Shock—loss of blood. Pretty girl." Fernandez looked a little sick. He drained the glass of water in front of him and wondered how he ever got involved in this kind of work.

"We don't know where this son of a—the perpetrator fired from, but we're combing the area for clues. We have police barricades on the street now. One round—probably the one that passed through the buttocks—was dug out of the sidewalk near where the victim was laying. Ballistics will call here with the report," Fernandez said and sat down.

No one spoke. Finally, Peterson looked at Hayes. "Is he a very bad shot or a very good shot?"

Hayes understood. He began slowly. "Well—it depends on the range, but I'd say he knew what he was doing. Breast, knee, foot, buttocks—he tortured her. Never took a shot at the male companion, I'll bet. Just watched his reaction."

Fischetti shook his head. "Sick. Sick."

"True," Hayes said. "He could be on that building across the street and fill this room with lead in less than five seconds—less than one second if he switches it to automatic."

"Automatic?"

"Most M-14s have an automatic capability."

"That's nice."

"We're definitely dealing with a psychotic," Peterson said, looking toward the open window.

The FBI man at the end of the table cleared his throat. Everyone looked up.

"Mr. Avery?" Peterson said.

Avery rose. "I don't want to break everyone's train of thought, but I might as well get this over with. It might be pertinent."

"Go right ahead."

The tall, good-looking man rose and fixed everyone with his steely blue eyes before he began. "As you know, I've been assigned as a special liaison to the N.Y.P.D. for the duration of this case. Officially, I'm only looking for a thief who stole some army property, while you're looking for a murderer. Normally, of course, the Bureau wouldn't go to the trouble of assigning a liaison to look for stolen government property, but the scope, however, if indeed that's what he's using, has a secret classification. We'd like to recover it. Unofficially, we'd like to help you with the murder end of it. The two are related, of course. If we recover the goods without the man, though, the Bureau and the army may be satisfied. They'd like the man, too, but the scope and whatever other munitions he has is the major concern right now. The man is obviously not a foreign agent, but we are concerned that the scope may fall into the wrong hands, as they say. There may be a lot of other equipment on the loose, as I have indicated. If we do recover the sensitive item or items, we will keep the case open, but we don't have the resources to sustain a special effort, as we are making now. We'd have to leave the apprehension of the perpetrator or perpetrators to local law enforcement agencies. Do I make myself clear?"

Not really, Hayes thought, as he nodded in agreement. He didn't like Avery and instinctively thought that the agent was not telling the whole truth.

"Very clear," said a voice from the shadow of the staircase. Everyone turned. Ryker strolled over and took a seat. He wore a tan suit, white shirt, and a maroon-and-blue tie, to no one's surprise. However, the suit he had on was clean, much to everyone's relief.

"What woke you?" Fischetti asked.

"Arm. Realized I needed a tetanus shot within twelve hours and an antibiotic. Went to Bellevue . . . overheard a nurse talking about the latest."

"Oh."

"So, continue," Ryker said.

Avery didn't fully understand the nature of the interruption, but he continued. "I have here this man Cyrus's medical records. The essence of it is this: He served in the Republic of Vietnam from May, 1973, to May, 1975. First six months as a regular infantryman. The last six months were spent as a LRRP sniper. In his last month of duty there—that's May, 1975—he caught a bullet in the head—frontal lobe—that's the personality center of the brain, of course. Apparently, a North Vietnamese anti-sniper squad got him. Left him for dead. From there to Oakland Army Hospital. Then to the VA Hospital. Complained of headaches. No motor damage—as coordinated as you or I."

Avery paused to collect his thoughts, then continued, "Some doctor up there began noticing that Cyrus was not acting normally. Talking to invisible friends. Remaining mute for days at a time. Refusing to eat. Eating spiders and the leaves off plants. This shrink decides to keep Henry around for a while, and that while was more than a decade."

"How come they kept him so long?" Ryker asked. "Especially since around here they let ax-murderers go over the weekend."

"Cyrus tried to kill an orderly and a doctor up there," Avery said. "He was violent almost all the time. Until recently."

"So they let him go?"

"He seemed, if not cured, less violent than before."

"Less violent," Ryker said. "What'd he do before, eat his victims?"

Detective Fletcher came into the room wheezing his laugh. The laughter was general and nervous.

"No, officer," Avery said. "The psychiatrists at Oakland thought they had him calmed down and allowed him into the minimum security wing of the hospital."

"Where he promptly broke out, came to New York, and started shooting people," Ryker said.

"Where'd he get this hot-shit, high-powered scope and M-14?" Ryker asked, before Avery had a chance to say anything else.

"There was a robbery at one of the army's weapon testing centers in Topeka," Avery said. "Several scopes and other items were stolen."

"Other items?"

"Classified, I'm afraid," Avery said smoothly. "You can buy an M-14 in any big gun shop."

"Did Cyrus rob the testing center?"

"We're not sure."

There was silence. Then the phone rang, and Peterson picked up the receiver.

He spoke for a second, then replaced the receiver and he turned to the group. "Crime Lab. Ballistics says the bullet from the FDR Drive occurrence and the bullet tonight match. I guess we figured that. Fernandez?"

"Yes, sir?"

"Go downstairs. Get on the horn and see what progress we're making."

Fernandez left. Avery announced that he was finished and laid the file in front of Peterson. "I'll be staying at the Sheraton Hotel. During the day, when I'm not here or in the field, I can be reached at the FBI office at Twenty-six Federal Plaza. Extract what you want from these files, and I'll pick them up in the morning. Good evening, gentlemen." Avery strode out of the room.

Hayes looked around. Nobody spoke. Fischetti called an all-night deli and ordered coffee and rolls.

Fernandez came up the stairs and broke the silence. "They found a shell casing seven-point-six-two millimeters at the base of a tree in the park. They're looking for more. Sent it to the lab for prints."

"How far from the victim?" Hayes said.

"About two hundred yards from the murder scene. They're searching the bush for more clues. There were a couple of good footprints in the mud, too."

"Footprints aren't really worth a shit," Ryker said.

After a time the rolls and coffee came. The men made small talk as they ate.

Peterson brushed some crumbs from his mouth and began one of his endless recapitulations. As he finished, he turned to Ryker. "Well—have any ideas?"

"Ideas? Detective work's over, Captain. We know who he is, and we found out within twenty-four hours of the first murder. Now it's only a matter of old-fashioned technique. Patrol cars, patrolmen, Anti-Crime units. Walk, talk, look, and listen. We all know the drill. If he's still in this city, he'll turn up. He's got to walk, breathe, eat and shit."

Peterson turned to Hayes, who had suddenly become the weapons and tactics expert since his talk with Lieutenant D'Angelo at the Academy. "How about—what did they call them in Vietnam—an anti-sniper squad?"

Hayes thought. "Maybe—let's get a hold of ESU again. They use Starlight scopes, by the way. Maybe station them on rooftops?"

"That's what I was thinking," Peterson cut in. "Ryker?"

"Okay. Maybe, but there's at least a half million rooftops in this city."

"He seems to like our section of town."

"He doesn't know the city," Ryker conceded. "Probably a little afraid of it, too, believe it or not. He just might stick around here. It's worth a try. We might try helicopters, too, I suppose."

"Right. Hayes, tomorrow you go over to ESU. I want a feasibility report on anti-sniper tactics by noon. I'll talk to the P.C., and we'll coordinate with Floyd Bennett Field. We should be able to squeeze at least four helicopters out of them. That's all we can do tonight, gentlemen. See you in the morning."

Everyone rose. Ryker spoke. "Wait. How about this guy's sister in Coffeyville, Kansas? Why don't we lean on her a bit? I'm willing to bet she has contact with her brother."

"The Coffeyville Police and the FBI are going to see her tomorrow. The FBI is getting a court order for a tap on her phone. I'm sure that's all we can do. See you in the morning."

Hayes was alone with Ryker. He got up and quietly pulled down the four window shades in the room.

Ryker looked at his watch. "Ten to four. Time to catch a quick drink at McGlade's before closing time."

"No alcohol with antibiotics."

"Alcohol is the best antibiotic invented. Hey, what do you think of Avery?"

"There's something not quite right there. He's not

saying all there is to say. Do you think this guy Cyrus is a heavy-duty espionage guy?"

"I agree he's not telling us everything, but Cyrus is a punk. Can't be very important by himself."

"Part of something bigger?"

"I hope not. If the Feds want him very bad, they'll want first crack at him. *I* want first crack at him."

"You mean *we*—the Police Department, don't you?"

"I mean *me.*"

The following eight days brought six more murders to the fear-stricken city, all in or near the East Village. The sniper's perches were: another deserted tenement rooftop; the window of a deserted tenement; a tree in Tompkins Square Park and the last three—unknown. All the victims were young, blond girls with long hair. Everyone was duly outraged and screaming for police action. Craig Rogers was having a field day. The Police Commissioner was seen entering and leaving the Mayor's office at City Hall every morning. He did not look happy and he made sure no one who worked for him was happy either. The vortex of the whirlwind seemed to center around the Eighth Precinct station house. This decaying structure suddenly became the backdrop for dozens of news films. TV reporters would stand with their backs to the building across the street and bray into their microphones.

Upstairs, the conference room had been designated by the Police Commissioner as a separate headquarters and clearinghouse for the sniper's activities. Charts and maps covered the walls, and extra detectives were assigned. Young women, especially blond ones, stayed indoors after dark. The more adventurous blondes bought short dark wigs or had their hair dyed, causing a run on these wigs and services at local beauty aid establishments.

Craig Rogers even did a special on "anti-sniper hairdos." Blacks, Hispanics, and other dark-haired women commiserated with their fair-haired sisters, but went on enjoying the throbbing night life of the city with as much pleasure as before. Arthur Hayes's whore dyed her hair back to its natural black and cut it. She was miserable for days.

Labor Day weekend came and went without any killings. A cool, evening breeze began blowing down from Canada, presaging the coming autumn.

Hayes was packing his belongings into a duffel bag at his hotel room. Ryker and Lindly sat on his bed drinking beer. Lindly was drunk.

"I think you should stick around, kid," Lindly said.

"Sorry. The wife thinks I'm up to no good in the evil city."

"Well, you are."

"That's besides the point. The point is, I've got my feet on the ground now. I can commute like everyone else. I can't afford this anymore, either."

"Can't afford this fleabag?" Lindly was lying down, balancing his beer bottle on his stomach, laughing.

"Okay, okay. I miss my wife and kids. School's about to start, and I should be there to help."

"Blondes have more fun—until they cut their hair and dye it black."

"Lay off," Hayes said.

"Sorry. Listen, kid, I'm going home now, too. I've got my car. I'll drop you off in Queens on the way back to the Island."

"I'll take the train."

"You might get mugged at this hour. Come on, let me drop you off."

"Very funny. I'd walk before I got into a car with a drunk like you."

"I am drunk," Lindly admitted.

Ryker stood. "Give Hayes your keys. Hayes, go down to the station house and pick up his car. Meet us in front of this shithole in fifteen minutes. You can drive this derelict home, keep the car and pick him up in the morning. I want you both at the precinct by seven A.M."

"Hey, I'm a sergeant, too. Can't I give some orders?" Lindly asked.

"No."

"Oh."

Ryker turned to Hayes. "Go ahead. Settle the bill on your way. We'll take your shit down."

Hayes took the car keys, which Lindly had reluctantly placed on his stomach, and left.

The two cops followed a few minutes later, taking the elevator to the floor where Hayes's girlfriend had a room. She answered the door wearing her nightgown.

"Joe, look what I had to do to my hair! When are you guys going to catch . . ."

"Listen, Maureen. Hayes's going home tonight—to his wife and kids."

"I know," she said sadly.

"I'm going to say this once and once only. You will never see him again, under any circumstances. You will never write and never call his house or the precinct. Understand?"

"Sure, sure," she said, but she didn't look happy about it. "I know what happens when a pro tries to go a little straight. Just like in the movies. He's such a doll. Damn it, I'm young. I want a regular boyfriend—I don't want to go back on the street. . . ."

After awhile she said, "Joe—my man—he's been keeping away because Arthur is a cop—he'll kill me now."

Ryker knew her pimp, a tall black man with an unusually nasty disposition.

"You tell Floyd I'm handling your action from now on."

Ryker and Lindly stood silently until she nodded.

"Take it easy, kid," Lindly said.

"Sure. Thanks."

The two cops went downstairs. Out in front of the hotel, the men waited.

"Dumb fucking kid probably gave her his home address and phone number," Lindly said. "She has his last name, anyway. Never give a whore your last name. Hell, never give your wife your last name, she'll only make trouble."

That made Ryker think about the fight he had had with Ellie years ago, the fight about last names. She had wanted to keep her own, he wanted her to take his. She lost the argument; he lost her.

Lindly seemed more sober now. "Probably showed her pictures of his kids, too."

As they waited, a van from the Vice Squad rolled by.

"Pussy Posse," Lindly said. "These pros don't have it easy. Hassled by Vice, their pimps, their johns—"

"All jobs have their ups and downs."

"And ins and outs."

Hayes pulled up in Lindly's car. Lindly got in and the two men drove off.

Ryker considered going back upstairs. He needed a woman, and Maureen Malloy was good, as he remembered from the time he had her on the floor of Hayes's room. He hesitated a moment, then thought better of it. As he crossed the street, he turned around. She was standing in the window of her room. She waved. Ryker turned his back and walked off.

He turned on Sixth Street and began the trek to the station house. On his way, he stopped at one of the chain of Irish bars that dot the area and ordered a double bourbon. At seven-thirty P.M., the bartender turned on the television. Craig Rogers was doing another special on the sniper, who had by now gone through three name changes from "mad sniper," to "quiet killer," to "blond killer." Whether the "blond" referred to his victims or to the killer, Ryker didn't know or care. He ordered another double.

The television screen suddenly showed a picture of Cyrus. Ryker knew this was helpful. The bar became quieter. With Rogers's voice in the background, the picture of Cyrus was overlayed with combinations of black hair, mustaches, glasses and beards.

"I don't understand it."

Ryker turned to the voice at his elbow. "What?"

The man sitting next to him turned on his stool to face him. "Everybody in this city knows what he looks like. He's got to live someplace. How does he explain to a landlord or a desk clerk when he goes out with a different get-up every day? How's he tote that damned gun around every night? How's he pick his spots without anybody seeing him? How's he get away? How's he . . ."

"Lots of questions, Mac."

"What the hell are the cops doing?"

"Cutting their long blond hair." Ryker got off the stool and patted the man's bald head. "I wouldn't worry about it if I were you."

Ryker walked the remaining distance to the station house. Upstairs, he noticed his desk was occupied by one of the newly assigned detectives. The man had his feet on the desk. Ryker walked over; the detective hurriedly got to his feet and found a new desk. Fischetti called to him. "Giving the reinforcements a hard time?"

"Do we need all these new people around here?"

"Come on. We've been through that. It's all eyewash for the papers and the Mayor. The P.C. insisted."

"If Peterson had any balls, he would have gotten rid of them long ago. Everybody's stepping over their dicks around here."

"Eyewash."

"Fine, but what we need is about a hundred plainclothes patrolmen walking the street. We need a dozen new detectives like I need a pair of tits."

"You're right, but we don't have any more patrolmen. Look, most of these guys are really working on their own cases from their old divisions. Nobody misses them much, but start to pull walking patrols off the streets from other precincts and you'd hear a howl from the neighborhoods that would bounce the mayor off his chair. This is a city of fear. Everybody's concerned with their own . . ."

"I'm just telling you how to catch this guy before he blows town. What's the latest on working the walking patrols that we have on two shifts and paying overtime?"

"P.C. called Peterson about that just an hour ago. City's broke. Mayor's summer clean-up of the Times Square area cost a fortune. Vice was working two shifts June, July and August."

"The Pussy Posse got the o.t. money, huh? Money badly spent, I'd say."

"Maybe. Anyway, money's tight."

Ryker walked over to his desk and pulled out a bottle of Jack Daniels. He sat down and drank from the bottle as he went through his paperwork.

NINE

Henry Cyrus lay in the sparse grass in Riverside Park. He carefully parted the vegetation and gazed down the open slope ahead of him. Halfway down the slope was the Henry Hudson Parkway, which was a continuation of the elevated West Side Highway that ended at Seventy-second Street. Beyond the Parkway was the Hudson River, sparkling with the reflected lights of both shores. Next to him was a long white box with the word "Macy's" printed in silver on its lid. The box had once contained some of the dark clothing he had purchased after the Washington Square Park shooting. Now it contained the reason he had to buy those new clothes.

Brooding, he lay on his stomach and played with the grass.

"Damn, they sure got on to us fast enough. Think they're so damn smart. Well, if they're so damn smart, why ain't they caught us yet, Mikey?"

Cyrus reflected sadly that virtually every one of his potential prey had disappeared from the streets after dark. He had wandered further uptown in hope of finding fresh hunting grounds. Instead, to his dismay, he found that he was on the edge of Harlem. He had walked toward the Hudson River on One Hundred Twenty-second Street and found himself facing Grant's Tomb. He stared at the marble structure for a time, then passed through the grounds of the Tomb and came to rest where he was now lying. After dark, he decided, he would make his way downtown again to his lair.

"Damn strange city," he said, as he plucked at the grass. "Wish I knowed where some more white folks lived. 'Bout cleaned out the game down there. Wish I could talk to somebody 'ceptin' you, Mikey. Feller in that there deli-cat-something damn near recognized me the other day. Gonna buy a map tomorrow for sure. Map won't show where the white folks live, though."

He thought a moment, then smiled. "Like to be able to walk right up to an old policeman and say, 'Excuse me, Mr. Policeman, can you tell old Henry how to get to where the white folks live in this here town?' " He chuckled softly. "Feller in a bar last week—asked him where the girls were. 'Upper Eastside, son,' that's what he said. 'Girl-ghetto on the east side—lots of secretaries, models, stewardesses for a young buck like you.' Tomorrow we'll walk into the sun and see what we can find, old buddy. Nothing but niggers around here. No more askin' nobody nothin' now with my face all over the place."

Cyrus looked at his watch. Nine P.M. He got up to leave. As he stood, he noticed the lights of a boat coming down the river toward him. He opened the Macy's box and removed the scope. Without mounting it, he held it up and flipped the switch.

"Damn near a mile—fifteen hundred, two thousand yards. Maybe a thousand, twelve hundred yards when she comes abreast. What the hell, ain't bagged nothin' in days."

He quickly assembled the rifle, knelt, and took aim. As the boat drew opposite him at about one thousand yards, he could see that it was an excursion boat. He could make out a few heads bobbing on the open aftdeck and faces pressed to the glass-enclosed foredeck.

"Shit, can't see nobody good."

Suddenly, he swung the gun up to the wheelhouse. He jammed a full magazine of twenty tracer rounds into the well and flipped the selector switch to "automatic." He took a deep breath, squeezed the trigger back, and held it. At a cyclic rate of fire of more than seven hundred rounds a minute, it took less than a second and a half to send ten rounds down range. He exhaled, drew a breath, and squeezed again until the gun clicked empty. The orange tracers made beautiful arcs as they sailed silently across the night sky, their long trails reflected in the smooth waters of the Hudson.

In the wheelhouse of the Circle Line tour boat, the first mate, who had the helm, caught a movement out of the corner of his left eye and turned. Suddenly, the small enclosure was a whirlwind of splintering glass and wood. The mate pitched sideways, and the wheel spun crazily. The captain, standing behind him, caught three bullets in the head and neck. He fell out of the door, down the catwalk, and crashed, dead, to the deck below. Most of the sightseers had pressed to the port side of the glass-enclosed foredeck when the tour guide had announced over his megaphone that the skyscrapers of Manhattan were coming into view. The second burst raked the foredeck as the astonished passengers watched the orange streaks coming at them. Soon, the deck of the tour boat was awash in blood and glass.

Cyrus stood. He could see the large boat start to veer to starboard. Then, as he watched, the current began to move it to port, toward the near shore, about four hundred yards from where he was standing. He wanted to stay and see it beach itself, but he knew better. Suddenly, he heard a voice behind him and spun around.

Damn! I shouldn't have used them damn tracers. Dead giveaway, he thought.

He jammed a new magazine of non-tracer rounds into the gun well and sprayed the vegetation in front of him. A scream, then excited shouting pierced his quiet perch. He quickly packed the rifle, gathered up the box and began the long run south through the bush. Riverside Park stretched for two more miles to the south and ended at Seventy-second Street. Cyrus made the distance in less than fifteen minutes. He passed several joggers and dog walkers on the way, but he kept his distance, and they didn't seem to pay any attention to him. He could hear sirens on the streets to his left as he ran. At the end of the park on Seventy-second Street, he stopped and caught his breath. His crew-cut brown wig had come askew, and he straightened it. He put on a pair of horn-rimmed glasses and began walking quickly and purposefully across town. He entered Central Park at its Seventy-second Street entrance. In ten more minutes he would be safe in his treetop lair, lashed to the branch of a huge old oak tree, almost a hundred feet from the ground. It had been a frustrating night, and he wanted sleep.

At five minutes to eight the following morning, Peterson had assembled more than twenty detectives in the conference room of the Eighth Precinct station house. Also present was John Avery, the FBI man. The men sat around the long table or sat on the window-sills, drinking coffee. At eight o'clock, the Police Commissioner strode in, followed by a half dozen other men, police and civilian. Everyone rose. Without formal introductions, the Commissioner waved them into their seats and began speaking. He had just come from an early morning meeting with the mayor, he said, and the mayor was "extremely concerned" over the nature of last night's killings. Ryker thought the P.C. looked like a man who had just had his butt chewed out pretty good. When he was through, the Commissioner wished them "good luck" and left. Two of the civilians with him remained behind.

Peterson rose and began one of his famous recapitulations. It seemed to Ryker that he started with the murder of Abel by his brother, Cain, and worked forward until he got to last night's occurrence. Peterson concluded by saying, "A potential witness who saw the tracer rounds coming from the bushes and ran over to investigate was killed. He was an elderly black man—probably didn't recognize the tracer streaks for what they were, and heard no noise because of the silencer." He paused and drank a glass of water. "The two other crewmen on board were apparently terrified of going back into the wheelhouse. The boat foundered offshore at about One Hundred Ninth Street. A passing Port Authority tug pulled it into the Parks Department dock at One Hundred Thirty-first Street. The wounded were evacuated to nearby hospitals. There were eight dead and six wounded. Any questions?"

A detective rose. "How do we know it was the same guy? The MO is different. And it was uptown this time."

"It's the same guy. Ballistics has the slugs found in the bodies. Same guy, all right."

"How about the shell casings?"

"Right: The police up there recovered almost forty of them. Apparently, he didn't have time to retrieve them. As was the case with the ones found at the Washington Square Park shooting, the prints on them were pretty bad. The shell is too small to get a whole print. Also, there were other prints on the casings. A lot of people could have handled those rounds before they found their way into a magazine."

"Why did he change his MO?" another detective asked. "Doesn't he like blonds anymore?"

"That's one of the things we're here to discuss. First, however, Dr. Wasserman, from Bellevue Medical Center, would like to say a few words."

Wasserman, a small, intense man of forty, stepped to the head of the table. He had been one of the men left behind by the Police Commissioner.

"Thank you, Captain. The Commissioner has asked me to say a few words to you about this suspect's brain impairment, which I have gleaned from his Army files and from conversations with some neurosurgeons at the Oakland Army Hospital and psychiatrists at the VA Hospital there. The Commissioner thought it might be useful to you to have these facts as a background for your investigation."

By his demeanor and tone of voice, it appeared to Ryker that he didn't think a bunch of cops could find this useful at all. Ryker didn't like doctors.

Wasserman read from a piece of paper. "As is well known, trauma of any kind to the brain, such as would result from a bullet wound, can result in a condition known as acute brain syndrome. Simply put, this is a result of diffuse, sometimes temporary, and reversible impairment of the brain. Often, this state is seen with hallucinations, delusion, and abnormality of behavior. Any questions so far?"

Lindly rose from the windowsill. "Doctor, his files mentioned that there was apparently no motor damage. Could you comment?"

Wasserman regarded him coolly for a moment, then answered. "Yes. When the damage is confined to the frontal lobe, no motor damage is usually evident. In other words, the subject's coordination and physical abilities may be quite normal." The doctor began picking up his papers as though to leave.

Another detective rose. "Dr. Wasserman, how about his intelligence and reasoning powers?"

The doctor slipped the files into a portfolio and looked up. "Again, if only the frontal lobes were affected, as seems to be the case according to the Army, there would normally be no impairment of his intelligence—such as there was—before the trauma. In English, he's as smart or as stupid as he was before he took that slug in the head. I should qualify that by pointing out that personality disintegration, if it develops enough, can appear to be, or in some cases lead to, loss of intelligence. If there are no other questions—I have an extremely busy day. No? Then, good day."

The doctor turned, gave Peterson a forced smile, and left.

Peterson stood, gave the retreating back a "thank you" and introduced Dr. Feld, an elderly psychiatrist, also from Bellevue. Feld seemed to love his subject and, in contrast to Dr. Wasserman, wanted to talk endlessly about it. After forty-five minutes, he smiled at his audience and concluded, "This guy is nuts."

Feld got a round of playful applause from the cops and seemed to enjoy it.

"Why does he only take out blondes?" Ryker asked. "Except, of course, for the Circle Line boat."

"I've already told you," Dr. Feld said. "He's nuts."

There was no laughter this time, so Feld elaborated. "According to his psychiatrist in California, the patient may have latent sexual feelings for his mother, who I believe was blond."

"Or his cocker spaniel who was also blond," Ryker snorted. "You really believe that some guy decided to shoot people because he's always wanted to rip a quick piece off his mother?"

"I . . . the psychiatrists in California may be wrong, sir," Dr. Feld said with dignity. "Psychiatry is an inexact science, at best. An art, really. Who knows what his real motives are?"

"Who cares?" Ryker said. "Unless they help us catch this scumbag, it's all a bunch of sh—"

"Thank you, Dr. Feld," Peterson broke in, and the psychiatrist left quietly.

Peterson now turned to the detective who had asked the question about the killer's new Modus Operandi. "To answer your previous question about the perpetrator's new MO, I'll turn it over to a man who has had the most intimate involvement in this case from the beginning, and has a profound knowledge of psychiatry, Sergeant Joe Ryker."

Ryker unexpectedly found himself the center of all eyes. He got up from his chair.

"Well, Captain Peterson's done such a fine job of recapitulating the past that I have nowhere to go but through my crystal ball into the future." A few men laughed, but most looked at Peterson, who did not seem to enjoy the remark. Ryker continued. "Okay. The new MO. It seems to me that this guy left our precinct area because it was either getting too hot for him, or because his specific type of victim—his game—was disappearing from the streets. Probably both. So, he doesn't know the city well and he wanders uptown. Probably used Riverside Park as a likely avenue of travel if he didn't want to walk the streets. He winds up in west Harlem. Not too many blondes there."

A few of the men laughed. A black detective smiled, "Yeah, and it sure felt different seeing someone getting picked on because their hair was *blond.*"

Ryker continued. "Well, I think he may go back to picking on whitey again. I think this thing in Harlem was a fluke. Apparently, what happened was that he got pissed off—hadn't killed in days. Took a walk. Wound up in Harlem. No blondes, right? Saw this boat and opened fire with full automatic. Sort of a way to release tension. Then, as the captain said, he ran back south through Riverside Park. At least five witnesses saw a man with a box, running south. He had a crew-cut—a wig, no doubt."

"Where did he run to?" Peterson asked, rhetorically. "That's what we'd all like to know."

"The park."

"*What* park?"

"Central Park, of course," Ryker said, as though everyone should know.

"How do you know?"

Ryker turned to Hayes. "Let's recapitulate, OK?"

Hayes stood uneasily. This was the biggest single group he had ever addressed. He looked around and began. "It's the only thing that makes any sense. This guy spent a lot of time in the jungle. Also, he's from a rural area. Apparently, he can't seem to get around the city, right? Maybe the first week or so he sleeps in alleys and doorways. Eventually, he discovers Central Park. Over two square miles of woods and fields right in the heart of the city. He's lived in a far more hostile environment, remember, so he feels at home in the park. He makes it his base camp."

"What the hell is more hostile than Central Park after dark?" one of the cops asked.

"It's not hostile to him," Hayes continued. "You can bet he shimmies between a rock fissure, crawls under some dead leaves, or ties himself to a tree every night. That's how they slept in Nam when they were on recon patrol."

"You're telling us he lives on nuts and berries?"

"No, but I'll bet he does find some pickings that way. He buys hot dogs, Cracker Jacks, peanuts, ice cream, and junk from the pushcart vendors in the park during the day. If you've ever noticed, they hardly ever look up when they're serving you. Anyway, this guy has about a dozen disguises."

"Where does he spend the day?"

"Right in the park. On the Green, the Sheep Meadow, the Great Lawn. Sometimes there're thousands of people lying on the grass there. Lots of them sleep with newspapers over their faces."

"How does he stay clean—presentable, so the cops won't roust him as a derelict?"

"Fundamental field sanitation. He practiced it in Nam. At night he washes and shaves in the pond, the lakes, the reservoir. Keeps all his gear compact in plastic bags and such. Just like in Nam. In short, the guy is a woodsman—a jungle fighter. This city is his jungle now."

There was a long silence in the room. The assembled detectives were letting Hayes's words sink in. If what he said were true, they all knew that they were up against something quite different from their usual urban police work. Their routine was based on address checking, apartment door knocking, phone tips, cab driver tips, landlord tips, snitch tips, loose bar talk, and all the other tried and true methods of detecting in a big city. They'd even dealt with urban guerillas on occasion, but a jungle guerilla in the heart of Manhattan was something else.

Finally Peterson spoke. "What happens when winter comes?"

Ryker answered. "He's gone. As soon as the leaves start falling and the people start thinning out in the park, he's gone. We have about another four weeks, at most."

Peterson looked thoughtful. "Okay. We don't have anything else. If all of what you say is in fact the case, we have our work pretty much cut out for us. I'll talk to the P.C. We'll get the park saturated with plainclothes patrolmen. Also you men should spend as much of your non-office hours as possible in the park. Dress casual. Maybe we'll even get some of our people to man pushcarts. I assume we'll only have a chance to nab him during the day."

"That's right," Ryker broke in. "We can forget him at night. He probably looks like a bush or a tree after dark. There is a chance, though, that we can pinch him on his way to his hideout." Ryker thought a moment. "What I'm worried about is that we won't find his cache when we find *him*. Without that gun, if you think about it, we don't have a fucking thing on him if he doesn't confess."

Peterson turned to Ryker and said something that Ryker would remember later. "Don't worry about evidence. Let's just catch the guy."

Ryker and Hayes spent the next several days in Central Park. At one point, they passed within thirty feet of the killer, who was sleeping on a high flat rock, with a newspaper over his face. Several hundred other people were doing the same thing in the fading

September sunshine, so he attracted no particular attention.

That night, a pretty twenty-year-old blond nurse from Roosevelt Hospital was torture-shot to death as she passed through busy Columbus Circle, at the southwest corner of Central Park. Hundreds of horrified onlookers hit the ground as they realized what was happening. The girl's body jerked and moved across the pavement as twelve bullets found their mark. This was a record number as the newspapers pointed out; it was also the most brazen of all the shootings so far. The girl's white uniform was completely crimson with blood. It came out through the newspapers that the nurse wasn't even a real blonde. She had donned the blond wig at the hospital after work. She jokingly took bets that she could walk crosstown to her apartment on the east side with it on. Her fellow workers, including doctors and technicians, playfully took the bet. They won.

The next morning, the FBI man, Avery, called Peterson and requested a meeting in Peterson's command center. The time was set for ten A.M.

At ten A.M., Avery walked into the station house with a very pretty suntanned blonde on his arm. She was about thirty years old, Ryker noted as he looked up from his desk. She looked like a kid but carried herself as though she were older. Her long straight hair hung down almost to her waist. Ryker knew, of course, this had something to do with the Cyrus case. He also knew that Peterson was becoming very secretive when Avery was around. He had been left out of too many closed-door meetings the last few weeks. Ryker got up and strode across the room, reaching the conference room door before Avery and the blonde. He opened the door for them and followed the pair inside.

Fischetti was talking to Peterson as the three of them entered. They stopped speaking and before they could say anything, Ryker sat down. Peterson now had the choice of ordering Ryker out or being diplomatic and avoiding a confrontation. He rose and said, "Please come in." Ryker was already in and lighting a cigar.

Avery didn't particularly want Ryker there but said nothing. Instead he said, "Gentlemen, may I present Captain Charlotte Cormier, United States Army."

Peterson and Fischetti stood. Ryker remained seated. Everyone else sat down, and Avery turned to the pretty captain. "Why don't you begin, Captain?"

The woman crossed her shapely legs and looked into the eyes of the men around her.

"Well, then, here it is. I've been stationed in Europe these past two months, or I would have come forward earlier. It was just last week that I heard about these awful killings here. I'm a native New Yorker myself by the way." She spoke in a very professional voice, but Ryker saw nothing but sex in her lustrous eyes. They were green like his own.

"I used to work in the neurological ward at the Oakland VA Hospital. I knew Henry Cyrus there for about nine months. Henry was a particularly pathetic case—introverted, subject to rages and catatonic comas—I felt sorry for him, so I had intercourse with him a few times after he was well enough to take it." She had said it so matter of factly that the men almost missed it. Fischetti felt like someone hit him with a hammer.

She went on. "I sometimes do that with the patients —it relieves a lot of their tension, you understand. I do it only with the ones who have full use of their mental faculties. In cases of motor damage—that is, paralysis, where the patient can't have normal intercourse—I find that digital or oral stimulation will achieve ejaculation in most cases. Now, this is not standard operating procedure, I should point out, but some nurses do it, especially in cases where the patient can't masturbate himself." Fischetti knew he was turning a little red and cursed himself for it.

"Sometimes, of course, the patient becomes emotionally attached. Henry was like that. He was quite pleasant, but I make it a practice not to see any patient outside the hospital. Anyway, he kept asking me if he could go to my apartment in town. When I refused, he felt rejected.

"Well, one night he was wandering around—he was really quite well at the time, I thought—and he saw me draw the curtains around a patient's bed—a nice young boy with partial paralysis due to a truck accident. I was helping this boy masturbate when Henry came rushing through the curtains. It took four orderlies to strap him down. The poor spinal patient—it set him back a few weeks. Anyway, I try to make each patient feel like he is the only one, but they talk of course and some of them become extremely jealous. What I'm doing for them becomes counterproductive at that point and I break it off slowly."

Ryker felt like saying, "What, their dicks?" but refrained.

Charlotte Cormier gave a long sigh and said, "So I feel that perhaps I had something to do with this awful obsession he has with murdering blond girls."

"Could be," Ryker said sarcastically.

Avery spoke. "We're not here to comment on Captain Cormier's method of therapy—and so that you don't think it was only this incident in the hospital that scrambled his brains . . ." He threw a piece of paper on Peterson's desk. ". . . this is an FBI report gathered from his hometown. It seems he had a girlfriend—long blond hair—before he went into the service. When he wrote to her from Oakland, he found that she had married and moved away. His sister says he took it very hard."

Ryker looked at Charlotte Cormier. "Captain Cormier . . ."

"Call me Charlie." She smiled.

Ryker couldn't see it. "Captain Cormier—you didn't come all the way from Europe to tell us you feel responsible—you could have put that in a letter."

"I don't feel entirely responsible," she shot back. "But I'm here to offer my help. If you want, I'll go on radio, TV, newspapers—anything you want, if it can be of assistance. I think I may be able to get him out in the open for you."

Peterson looked at Avery.

"It's okay with me," the FBI man said.

For the next two days, the newspapers, radio, and television were filled with appeals by Captain Charlotte Cormier to ex-PFC Henry Cyrus, saying, in effect, that he should stop shooting at people—that she loved him and that she would help him. The news media was always sure to include Captain Cormier's New York address as, "The Plaza Hotel at the corner of Fifty-ninth Street and Fifth Avenue." This sounded as strange to native New Yorkers as saying that the Fifty-ninth Street Bridge was at Fifty-ninth Street. Everyone knew where the Plaza was. But Henry Cyrus was not a real New Yorker.

He heard Charlotte Cormier's voice for the first time from a nearby transistor radio while he was lying on the grass near the carousel in Central Park. In twenty minutes—at three-twenty-two P.M. to be exact—he was standing in Grand Army Plaza at the southeast corner of Central Park, looking up at the ornate old hotel. Within two minutes, he was surrounded and handcuffed by sixteen FBI agents. He offered no resistance.

Charlotte Cormier checked out of the St. Regis Hotel where she had actually been staying, and flew back to Europe that evening.

It was the biggest anticlimax to the largest manhunt in New York City's history.

Ryker was blazing mad.

TEN

Ryker paced the floor of the squad room, muttering to himself. Hayes looked perplexed. He had brought Ryker the news that Cyrus had been picked up and thought his partner would be happy for a change.

"What's eating you, anyway?"

"Hayes, you're an asshole."

"Why?"

"It was a Federal bust. We're never going to see that cocksucker."

"So, he's caught. That's what counts."

"Fucking Peterson swore they'd tail this guy until he went for the rifle. You're a smart kid sometimes—do you think we'll ever find that gun if it's in the park?"

"No." Hayes looked troubled. "Shit, it could be buried, wrapped in plastic."

"Exactly. We've got no real evidence against the bastard. He'll never go to trial for murder."

"What?"

"You heard me. The Feds are more concerned with

their fucking Starlight scope than they are about anything else. Henry Cyrus will get lost in the shuffle somewhere or some smart-ass lawyer will make a deal," Ryker said, slamming his fist on the desk.

"Why would Captain Peterson . . ." Hayes began.

"Politics," Ryker growled. "Only it's not just Peterson. It went higher than that. Something really smells here."

Fischetti had been listening. "Easy, Ryker. There's probably a perfectly good explanation for why they collared him."

"What?"

"Well, I think the P.C. thought it over and got scared that Cyrus might lose the tail. He probably had nightmares about telling the mayor how Jungle Jim slipped through our fingers."

"Bullshit. That gun was the whole case. Something is really fucked-up here. Why were all the guys who collared him Feds? I'll tell you why: so that we wouldn't get word that it was going to be an arrest instead of a tail."

"You sound paranoid," Fischetti said.

"I just don't understand it. How often does a suspect slip a tail? It's just not correct police procedure to nab a suspect like that. What do we really have on old Henry?"

The phone rang. Fischetti was glad he didn't have to answer that question.

Downtown, on the twenty-eighth floor of Twenty-Six Federal Plaza, Special Agent Avery was feeling in an expansive mood.

"You know, Carl," he said to Captain Peterson, "I want to thank you and the P.C. for the great job you did on this case."

Peterson was nervous. He didn't say anything.

"Cyrus will be up here in a minute, after he's seen our pet judge across the street," Avery continued. "And we'll get what we want from him."

"It's most, uh, irregular," Peterson said.

"It's national security," Avery replied.

At the Eighth Precinct, Lieutenant Fischetti rounded up his men.

"Come on, Ryker," he said. "We've put him away, that's what counts. Why are you taking it so personally?"

"It's not personal. It's professional. My profession is to put lunatics like him away. I worked hard on this case, and some asshole stepped in and blew it."

Fischetti nodded. After a few seconds, he looked around the room. "Hey, this looks like the city morgue. Let's go down to McGlade's. We do have *some* reason to celebrate. At least the pressure is off. It's my treat."

Ryker reluctantly agreed to go along. As the party of four cops walked on Sixth Street, they passed a newsstand. The newsdealer was hawking a late-edition *New York Post* that carried the headline, SNIPER CAUGHT.

Inside the bar, the men took a round table in the corner. Ryker, Hayes, and Littel drank bourbon, while Fischetti ordered Scotch. He had left a message with the desk sergeant and expected more cops would show up as they found out there was a celebration going on. After a half hour of drinking and speculating on the outcome of the case, Lindly showed up with his regular partner, Wilkinson. So did Ralph Fletcher, his bald head covered by a fedora. As the liquor unwound the men, the party became more spirited. The bartender and some other patrons, realizing what the celebration was about, sent over several rounds of free drinks. Fernandez wandered in at about ten-thirty and by eleven, everyone was very drunk. The conversation turned back to the Cyrus case at eleven-thirty, after they had all watched the television news.

Lindly: "Hot shit, that bitch blowing in like that. That nurse, I mean."

Littel: "We're jumping through our asses to find this prick, and this bitch says old Henry liked her blow jobs or something, and she'd nab him for us."

Fernandez: "Love, true love."

Fischetti: "Shit—we would have grabbed him, anyway. We had that park covered from end to end."

Hayes: "The fucking news is giving all the credit to the Feds. That asshole Avery didn't do shit. This cunt just walks into the FBI office . . ."

Ryker: "Where the fuck's the gun, Fischetti?"

Fischetti: "How the fuck should I know?"

Ryker: "That still leaves the asshole alive."

Fischetti: "So what? What do you care? Just do your job. You're not the judge and jury, too."

Ryker: "Why didn't we tail him? Something smells here."

Fletcher: "It's you, Ryker. You smell like a fucking dog shit–eater to me."

Ryker: "If I had your nose, I'd be able to smell every armpit east of the Mississippi River."

Fletcher: "You'd love it, ya shithead."

Ryker: [Burp]

Fischetti: "You think something stinks here, Ryker? Blow him away."

Ryker: "Fuck you, fishhead. Candy-ass, asshole, ass-kisser."

Patron: "Hey! There's a fight. Get the cops."

Bartender: "They *are* the cops."

* * *

At seven-thirty A.M. a hand-picked task force of city detectives, uniformed officers, park rangers, and guys with long, nail-studded poles and canvas sacks began combing Central Park for Cyrus's M-14. It was a beautiful, warm fall day, the kind of day that cried out to be enjoyed—unless it was ruined by a hangover. Ryker believed that death would be a just reward after an entire night of boozing it up with Hayes and Fletcher. His mouth tasted like the inside of a Roach Motel, his head pounded, his stomach heaved, and the goddamned birds sounded like a brass band to his sensitive ears.

Lieutenant Fischetti, who seemed totally unaffected, gave them the briefing. "As you know, we've got more than a hundred men, uniformed and plainclothes, ready to turn the park upside down. The mayor has instructed the Parks Commissioner to lend us another hundred men. Each cop is paired off with one of these guys. The consensus seems to be that if he did hide it in Central Park and not someplace else, we'd still find it only by sheer luck. If it's someplace other than the park—forget it." Fischetti went on, "The Parks Commissioner and, for that matter, the Police Commissioner won't use a hundred men a day forever. We've got to find it quick. What's potentially worse, though, is that a lot of public-spirited types are joining in the search. The word, as they say, is out."

Ryker looked up from his thoughts. "That's all the fuck we need. With our luck, another psycho will find it."

"Could be," Fischetti agreed. "Want to hear the really bad news now?"

"Sure."

"Your buddy from WNYM—Rogers—has talked his station into offering a ten-thousand-dollar reward for the recovery of the weapon or information leading to its recovery. They're going to announce it tonight —another of Rogers's cheap gimmicks. Anyway, the P.C. is trying to get a court order to stop them, but it won't do much good. Once the reward offer is made, all the court orders in the world won't keep the loonies from tearing up the park. This will look like the biggest Easter egg hunt Central Park has ever had."

Ryker shifted his feet, crushing the grass. "There's only one person who knows where that gun is, and there's only one way to get him to show us."

Fischetti saw another scene coming. "Listen, the gun isn't everything."

"Bullshit. This was a classic case before somebody fucked it up. Locate the perpetrator—follow him—he leads us to evidence, a gun in this case. The prints on the gun and his possession of the gun link him solidly *to* the gun. Ballistics link the gun to the murder. Classic case. What did you do at the Police Academy—jerk off in the men's room all day?"

Fischetti sighed. "That's enough. I'm sick and tired of all this Monday morning quarterbacking. Let me ask you something: How do you know he'd have led us to the gun if the Feds hadn't snatched him?"

"I know he would. I'm as sure of it as I'm sure that this bastard will never go to trial. He'll be in the rubber room for a few years, then dumped on the streets."

"Well, uh . . ." Fischetti mumbled.

"That's it, isn't it?" Ryker said, sensing the opening and probing the lieutenant's uncertainty.

"Enough," Fischetti broke in. "If you have any more questions, speak to Captain Peterson. It's my job—our job—to find the rifle. That's all."

Ryker shut his mouth, but he wasn't through yet.

* * *

That evening, after a fruitless day in the park, Ryker went home to his cluttered apartment. A drunk was sleeping in the doorway, but Ryker was too tired to kick him out of the way. He just stepped over the man.

Upstairs, he unscrewed the cap on a bottle of Jack Daniels and took a swig. The sour mash felt sour going down. He wished he had someone to talk to, but the phone never rang and he was too proud to call Ellie.

At the Eighth Precinct, Captain Peterson was clearing out his papers. The hunt for Henry Cyrus was over and he was looking forward to getting back to his comfortable office at One Police Plaza. Field work was exciting for a time, but he wanted to get back to headquarters as quickly as possible. There was no telling who was trying to knife him in the back.

Peterson had just finished stuffing his black leather briefcase when Lieutenant Fischetti came into the room.

"Can I ask you a question, Captain?"

"Shoot."

"What the hell happened with the Cyrus bust? How come the Feds grabbed him?" Ryker's persistence had worn Fischetti down.

Peterson got up and closed the door. Then he said, "Lieutenant, I trust you can keep your mouth shut."

"Yes, sir."

"Then you might as well know the whole story. Cyrus will probably get off," Peterson said.

"What?"

"It was a bad bust."

" 'Cuz the Feds fucked it up?"

"Yes and no. There's national security involved here—the scope," Peterson said.

"How about the security of the people on the street?" Fischetti asked.

"What can I tell you?" Peterson asked, then answered his own question. "It had to be done. The Feds think Cyrus is part of a conspiracy. They think he's in with a bunch of gun runners operating in this country and overseas. It's not the guns so much, it's the technology they're stealing—like the Mark V Scope. It's national security," Peterson repeated.

"It's a crock and you know it," Fischetti said. "What are they doing with him, as if I didn't know?"

Peterson looked uneasy. "That's really not our concern. The point is, if we hit him with murder one and it sticks, he'll be sent to prison or the loony bin for life. He'll have no reason to cooperate with the Feds, and they'll have nothing to offer him. This way we grab him, the killings stop for us, the pressure is off, and the FBI takes over. Very simple. Everybody is happy."

"Except the people who got killed. Except the D.A., who probably doesn't know a fucking thing about this phony deal."

"Lieutenant, these deals, as you call them, are arranged every day between cooperating law enforcement agencies. You know that as well as I do."

"It's lousy, anyway. It stinks," Fischetti said, using Ryker's term.

Peterson was red. "Wait a minute, Lieutenant. . . ."

"And what happens to him when the government gets him?" Fischetti said. "He sings. Only the government never brings up the fact that he's loony. That would destroy his credibility as a witness against the rest of the ring. They make a deal with him if he sings. He gets five to ten in a Federal pen. He's out in three to four."

Fischetti and Peterson stared at each other for a long moment.

Fischetti spoke again. "Including the FDR Drive and the excursion boat, we have almost fifty dead."

Peterson turned and faced the window. "I had absolutely no choice. The government feels this gun ring is important."

"Don't start waving that national security crap in my face. You're a cop, Carl. This city is your responsibility. Let the FBI worry about their own problems. It was a lousy deal, Captain."

"It was. But I had no choice," Peterson conceded.

"Anyway, how do we really know there's a conspiracy? How do they know that he's in on it? He's had his brains scrambled. Think he remembers? Maybe he was only a customer."

Peterson was still staring out the window. "Lot of questions. I don't know. They didn't tell me everything," he said, almost in a whisper.

Fischetti felt he had been used; he knew he had been lied to, and there wasn't a damn thing he could do about it.

For the next few weeks, private citizens frantically searched Central Park. They had as many motives for joining in the search as they had ideas on where the gun was hidden. They brought spades, long steel probes, and even sophisticated metal detectors. The police spent as much time chasing the searchers off as they spent searching for the rifle. A local radio station held a contest and asked its listeners to call in with ideas and theories on where a rifle could be hidden. Among the wilder ideas was a suggestion from a veterinarian that an elephant's rectum would accommodate something as big as an M-14. It turned out that an elephant's rectum *would* hold a rifle but that the elephants in the park zoo were clean.

Craig Rogers showed clips of the search nightly. The

police search, of course, was all show. It would be a miracle if the gun was found. The FBI, however, held their collective breath during the search; they wanted Cyrus for themselves. If he didn't go for the gun when he got out, that was all right, too. They felt he had a lot more munitions hidden someplace around Coffeyville, and he would surely lead them to that cache. With any luck at all, he would lead them to the conspirators, too.

Ryker went back to routine homicides. As the weeks dragged by, he became more and more convinced that Cyrus should pay for the murders that he committed. It became an obsession.

Cyrus's Legal Aid lawyer asked for and got permission for Cyrus's sister to visit him in the prison ward at Bellevue. The FBI was furious. They wanted to keep the killer completely incommunicado and made plans to transfer him to the nut house in Washington, where Cyrus would be fun company for John Hinkley. But it was nearing holiday time, and the paperwork was massive. The public soon forgot about Henry Cyrus and his trail of murder. New York was like that. The world was like that.

One day in late November, Joe Ryker walked up the cold granite steps of the WNYM building on Tenth Avenue. The pretty receptionist asked him his business.

"I have an appointment with Mr. Rogers."

Inside Rogers's wood-paneled office, the newscaster stuck out his hand and smiled, "What can I do for you, Sergeant?"

Ryker ignored his outstretched hand and sat down. Rogers expected some unpleasantness and waited for the worst, but Ryker just fixed his hard green eyes on him and said, "I'm here to make a deal."

"You've come to the right place."

"I think you have enough power, influence and money to pull this off."

"Pull what off?"

"How would you like a very good scoop?"

"That's my business." Rogers perked up.

"I want you to spring Henry Cyrus."

"What?"

"You offered ten thousand dollars for the recovery of the gun. You'll need ten thousand more to get him out."

"Why the hell should we want him out?"

"To get the gun."

"Oh. Is it legal?"

Ryker stood up to leave.

"Wait, wait," Rogers said. "There's a bigger story here than the recovery of the gun. You're not telling me everything."

"That's the story you'll have to settle for." Ryker was ready to go.

"If the police department doesn't know about this, who's going to follow Cyrus?"

"My partner and I. We're cops, remember?"

"How do we get him out?" Rogers asked. "Without going to jail ourselves?"

"You might want to check out this name," Ryker said, handing the newscaster a three-by-five file card. It read: Dorian Gillette.

"Who's this?"

"Never heard of him," Ryker said, walking out the door. "You've got sources, use them."

Two days later, near midnight, Ryker was in his apartment, cutting his toenails. It was an easy job because his toes poked through his socks. That reminded him he had to order another dozen wool socks, all black, so he'd have no trouble matching them. *Problems, problems,* he thought.

The phone rang. It was Craig Rogers's unmistakable voice.

"This is a friend," Rogers said. "You'll remember our conversation of two days ago, in my office."

"Is this Craig Rogers?" Ryker said slyly, laughing his ass off inside. His line wasn't tapped; he checked it twice a week.

"Shhh!" the newscaster said. "No names."

"Okay, Craig, I mean, okay. What's up?"

"Meet me in an hour," Rogers said. "At the bar next to my office."

"You mean Meehan's?"

"Shhh!"

"Okay, in an hour."

Meehan's was an Irish bar with an identity problem. It had once been a hangout for working men, then a newsman's dive. Late in life, the TV people moved in to give the place a midlife crisis—potted plants mixed in with dusty portraits of Saint Pat, *New Yorker* prints mingled with Guinness Stout signs and the clientele was part old-time boozers, part Perrier and white winos. Ryker hated the place.

Rogers was in a dark corner, the fur collar of his Chesterfield pulled up around his ears, as if everyone in the place didn't know who he was anyway. He was enjoying the hell out of the cloak-and-dagger, Woodstein–Deep Throat bit.

"Were you followed?" Rogers asked Ryker as he sat down.

"By the Emerald Society Marching Band, Craig. They'll be here soon to play a mazurka on your face."

"Be serious."

"I never joke," Ryker said. "J.D. rocks," he told a passing waitress.

"I met your man," Rogers whispered.

"I don't know who or what you're talking about. I'm only here to provide you with the background information you need to report on the Henry Cyrus case," Ryker said.

"Okay, have it your way. We're on for a week from today. Seven A.M."

"Can't hear a word you're saying," Ryker said. "Must be the noise in here."

"Come on, Ryker. . . ."

"No, you come on, Rogers. Anything you do is your own responsibility. I have nothing to do with it."

Rogers sighed. "I'll be there myself."

"You're too old and out of shape . . . for such an early morning jog."

"I'll send my associate."

"Send in the home team, coach. I'm out of here," Ryker said. The J.D. never arrived.

A bitter cold wind blew down Ninth Avenue as Ryker turned up his collar and walked to a nearby bar where Hayes was waiting for him. The bar, in what had once been the Hell's Kitchen section of New York, was suffering the same schizoid fate as Meehan's. Hayes sat at the bar and looked up nervously as Ryker entered.

"Well?"

"All set."

"Jesus Christ, I hope you know what you're doing."

"A man is springing old Henry, and if a couple of dedicated cops happen to see him, it's our duty to find out where he goes. Even if we're on vacation."

"Yeah, but this stuff with the FBI . . ."

"You don't know a thing about that. Forget it." Ryker ordered a double bourbon.

The following day, Ryker and Hayes started their long overdue vacations. Hayes told his wife a fantastic story about tracking mobsters and moved onto Ryker's threadbare couch. The following night, the phone rang. Ryker picked it up.

"Hi, Joe," his ex-wife said. "Did I catch you at a bad time?" She liked to say that, he knew, to see if he had a broad stashed in the apartment. He always said no, it wasn't a bad time, because he didn't bring hookers home with him.

"Yeah," he said. "I've got company."

"Oh, well, I'll hang up then," she said, waiting for him to say, oh, no, that's all right. This time he didn't.

"Good night, Ellie," he said. "I'll call you soon."

"She must be something," Ellie said. "Someone I know?"

"Good night," Ryker said, hanging up.

Hayes belched and scratched his belly. "Who was that? Some broad?"

"Not anymore."

In the freezing darkness of six A.M., Ryker and Hayes stood in front of Bellevue. At seven-thirty, Hayes became worried. Finally, from the dark recesses of the doorway, Ryker spotted Cyrus. Rogers's man was helping him on with an oversized yellow topcoat that he had brought along. The color was Rogers's idea, Ryker figured. Ryker thought Rogers was an asshole for thinking that he needed a yellow coat to tail Cyrus. In the streetlight now, the reporter quickly moved off, leaving Cyrus dumbfounded. He looked up at the buildings around him and made a few tentative steps down the sidewalk. Ryker couldn't help laughing.

"That silly bastard doesn't know what's happening to him."

"He sure don't like this cold," Hayes said.

The young reporter had walked around the block and came up behind the two cops. "Name's Winston," he said with a smile.

Ryker didn't turn around.

"That so?"

"What's he going to do?" Hayes asked.

"He doesn't know himself, yet."

As the sun started to creep into the canyons of Manhattan, Cyrus decided which way was north and started walking. The three men followed.

Two hours later, Cyrus was standing at the corner of Forty-second Street and Fifth Avenue shivering with cold. He had stopped a few people and asked directions along the way, but Ryker had kept up with him easily because Cyrus had avoided subways, buses and cabs. Apparently, he didn't know anything about public transportation, and that was a break for his pursuers. Like a good infantryman anywhere in the world, Cyrus was depending on his own two legs to move him from point A to point B.

Cyrus walked west on Forty-second Street, then turned into a Chock-Full-of-Nuts Coffee Shop. The cops knew that Cyrus was in more familiar territory now; if he got to the park, he'd be difficult to track.

"How much money did you give him, Winston?"

"Twenty dollars. That's what Mr. Rogers said."

The men watched from across the street, as Cyrus drank hot coffee and ate donut after donut.

"Why don't you run into that bar over there and get us all some hot coffee?" Ryker said to the reporter.

"I'll stick," Winston replied. He was told to expect a brush-off attempt.

The men shivered, stomped and froze for almost an

hour, then finally Cyrus came out, turned west again, then walked north on Eighth Avenue. At Columbus Circle, at the southwest corner of Central Park, he sat on a bench; the three men stood behind the Columbus monument and waited.

Hayes turned to his partner. "It must be in the park."

"Maybe. He won't make a move toward it until nightfall anyway," Ryker said. "Why don't you get us some coffee, Winnie?"

"I'll stick."

The men stood and waited as the hours dragged. Cyrus had gotten up several times to walk around. Once he walked into the park but only to urinate. The three men moved around the sides of the tall statue every time Cyrus took a walk around the plaza.

As Ryker stood with his back to the north side of the statue's pedestal, he realized that he was only a few yards from the spot where Cyrus had put twelve rounds through the nurse from Roosevelt Hospital. The sky started to darken and sleet began beating down on the frozen pavement. Hayes began to sneeze and cough.

"I wonder how long it'll be before they miss him." Hayes said.

"Soon," Ryker said, wiping the sleet from his eyes. "Real soon. Poor Henry, he doesn't like this weather one bit."

"I don't think much of it, either," Hayes said, coughing. "My balls are trying to crawl up into my belly." The reporter looked like he was going to fall over.

By five-fifteen, it was completely dark. Cyrus rose from the bench, put his hand on the low stone wall behind him and vaulted into the park.

ELEVEN

"Shit!"

The three men were so wet and tired that they hadn't noticed Cyrus slip over the wall. When Ryker glanced around the corner of the monument, he saw that his quarry was gone. He cursed and looked frantically around the square before shaking his companions and running over to the bench where Cyrus had been sitting. The handprint in the slush on top of the wall showed him where Cyrus had gone. The three men entered the park through an opening in the wall, where they spotted fresh tracks across the open field and followed slowly. After a few hundred yards, they entered an area of thickening vegetation, knelt and listened as the sleet beat furiously through the bare, frozen trees. Then they began following the footprints in the freezing slush.

Again, they broke into an open field. Ahead of them lay the Heckscher Playground; running with long, sure strides, like a wolf across the frozen field, was the silhouette of Henry Cyrus.

"Shit," Ryker said, noticing that Cyrus's overcoat was very dark now. "He's turned it inside out," he said with professional appreciation. Cyrus disappeared inside the tree line at the far end of the field, while his pursuers sprinted after him, using the intermittent cover of the playground. An oversized grouping of Alice in Wonderland characters added an unreal quality to the white ice field. The men entered the tree line about a minute after Cyrus. They crouched and listened. Hayes leaned over and whispered breathlessly into Ryker's ear. "He can't hear us in this sleet. Let's get closer."

Ryker nodded. The men moved forward. In a few minutes they passed through the small copse of trees and came upon the first transverse road through the park. They could see footprints leading across the road. Ryker had had enough training to know that this was a danger point. The close bordering trees on both sides of the road made the road itself a naked killing zone. If Cyrus were armed—and by now they couldn't be sure he wasn't—the three men would be dead before they got to the middle of the road. To assume that he was unarmed and that he didn't know he was being followed could be fatal.

Ryker led his two companions parallel to the road for a hundred yards. He had them cross one at a time. The men then doubled back and picked up the trail again. At the end of the cluster of trees, they came out onto The Green. Cyrus was crossing this big open field diagonally, heading toward The Mall; the men stood and watched. Suddenly, Ryker clenched his right hand into a fist and grabbed it with his left. He pivoted and drove his right elbow into Winston's solar plexus. The young man's eyes bugged out, and he pitched forward at the waist. Ryker brought the knife edge of his left hand down on his neck, and the reporter collapsed onto the icy earth.

"He should have gone for coffee."

Hayes stared. Ryker pulled a gun out of his coat pocket and checked out the mechanism. Hayes noticed that the gun was a cheap Saturday Night Special. Suddenly, Hayes realized that Henry Cyrus would not leave that park alive.

"Let's go."

Hayes hesitated.

"Move!"

Reluctantly, Hayes fell in behind his partner, and they began crossing the field. For the next hour, they worked their way north through the slush and ice. Hayes was in his element now. He had known about the tracking and stalking of game since he was a boy.

If Hayes was good, Cyrus was better. He had known for the last hour or more that he was being stalked. He also knew that whoever was doing the stalking was good—damned good. He knew that they must have been with him for some time before he became alerted to it. If he tried to shake his pursuers, he would give away the fact that he knew he was being followed. He was still unarmed and had only surprise on his side for the moment. He guessed he was being tracked by at least two men.

As Cyrus passed by the reservoir in the north of the park, Ryker and Hayes knelt in the last tree covering. Suddenly, Cyrus began to sprint around the reservoir. The two cops were in a dilemma. If they ran after him, he would know he was being followed; if they waited for him to disappear into the trees again, at the speed he was traveling now, they might lose him.

Cyrus reached the trees. Once within the covering, he increased his speed even more. As he passed a small sapling, he stuck out his right hand, grabbed it on the run and spun off the trail. He slipped and crawled a few more yards, then he reached through the freezing slush until he found a long thin piece of slate that he had left there that past summer. He grasped the slate and began digging frantically through the slush, through the dead leaf mat and into the soggy ground. A pair of squirrels watched him curiously. He could hear running footsteps coming toward him on the trail. They were getting very close now. At last, he reached a thick layer of polyethylene plastic, supported by cross-stakes. He slashed through the plastic with the slate and thrust his arm into the small hole. He groped furiously through his cache for a weapon. The footsteps were almost on him now.

The two cops overran Cyrus's trail and had to double back. Ryker knew there was something wrong. He could swear that he had heard another set of footsteps behind him through the wind and beating sleet. He spotted the place where Cyrus had turned off the narrow path and hesitated. Warning bells were ringing in his head; he pulled the Saturday Night Special from his pocket.

Cyrus's frozen fingers curled around a familiar cylinder-shaped object. This would have to do. He extracted his hand from the hole, pulled the pin on the black cylinder and heaved it in a long steep arc. The heavy concussion grenade seemed to hang in mid-air for a second, then the short-timed fuse popped and the grenade exploded in flight. The noise shattered the night air. Frozen blue ice rained down from the surrounding trees with a light tinkling sound.

The two cops were jerked off their feet and slammed back to the ground. The killer again rummaged through his cache, looking for his Colt .45. As his stiff fingers cocked the heavy gun, he heard the sounds of approaching footsteps. Taking a quick estimate of the situation, he figured that there were many cops and he felt too frozen and tired to make a stand. He thrust both arms into his hole and yanked at the long plastic-wrapped bundle that held his rifle. It was stuck. He could hear voices less than ten yards away. Reluctantly, he got to his feet and began sprinting west.

Ryker opened his eyes slowly. He could feel a steady thumping on his rib cage. Instinctively, he reached into his shoulder holster and drew out his .357 Magnum. A foot kicked it away. The thumping stopped. He wiped the driving ice from his eyes and looked up into the muzzle of a .38 Police Special. As he looked past the gun, he could make out the handsome features of John Avery, the FBI agent. Another man stood beside him. Ryker groaned and inclined his head. That's when he saw Hayes. Blood trickled from the young man's ears and nose; Ryker closed his eyes again.

"You're a bastard," Ryker said when he opened his eyes.

Avery got up from his chair and told the nurse to leave. He leaned over Ryker's bed. "I should have left you there."

"Why the fuck didn't you? We didn't need . . ." Suddenly, he sat upright. "Where's Hayes?"

"Behind the curtain. Unfortunately, he'll live. Minor concussion."

"Fuck you," Ryker said, but he was relieved and sat back. "Why were you kicking me, you prick?"

"I was trying to keep my feet warm. Listen, you're lucky he didn't toss a fragmentation grenade. If he did, we'd still be unstringing your guts from the trees."

"Fuck you." Ryker said again, then suddenly he realized he had a lot of questions to ask. "Where's Cyrus?"

"Gone. We recovered most of his cache."

"The gun?"

"Gone—scope, too."

Ryker stared up at the ceiling.

"We found a cheap Saturday Night Special, serial number filed off."

"So?"

"I don't think it was his."

"So?"

"Your P.C. wouldn't think too highly of you taking the law into . . ."

"Where am I?"

"You're supposed to say that as soon as you wake up."

"Where am I?"

"Roosevelt Hospital."

"How the fuck did he get away?"

"There were only three of us, smart-ass. I peeled one guy off to evacuate that reporter you fucked up."

"What reporter?"

"If you knew how close I came to leaving you there to freeze to death."

"Why were you following me?"

"It was a nice day. I decided to take a walk in the park."

"Prick."

"As you can probably figure out, we don't have anything on you. Or your friend Rogers and that orderly . . . what's his name?" Ryker was silent. He wasn't going to fall for that one.

"Yeah, Gillette."

"What the fuck are you talking about?"

"Okay, smart guy, but your ass is grass from now on and I'm the grim reaper. You have a lot of explaining to do to your people, too."

"I don't have to explain shit to anybody—and don't start telling me it was my fault. It was your fault from beginning to end."

"Okay. I'm not supposed to tell you this because of your delicate condition, but Cyrus blew away two cops tonight."

"Get out of here."

"Gladly." Avery turned and left.

Ryker lay motionless for a few minutes. Finally, he rolled unsteadily from his bed and made his way over to the wall locker. He got dressed, then looked around the small room for his guns, knowing they wouldn't be there. His badge and wallet were gone, too. He looked in on Hayes, who was either still unconscious or sleeping, then pulled the curtain around his own bed. He slipped quietly into the hall and down the elevator.

Outside the hospital, in the cold driving sleet, his head began to clear. He figured the time at between five and six in the morning, but he didn't know the day. He rubbed his beard and decided that he hadn't lost a whole twenty-four hours. This must be the morning after his chase through the park.

He walked all the way downtown through the storm, muttering and cursing to himself. He entered his empty apartment quietly, since the slightest noise gave him a searing pain that seemed to run from his ears through his brain and into his sinus cavities. From a hole in the wall, behind his dresser, he retrieved a .25 Beretta. Ryker looked at the small gun contemptuously. It was a woman's gun, but it was the only one he had in his cache at the moment. He also pulled out five hundred dollars he had stashed for emergencies and stuck it in his pocket.

Cursing Avery, Ryker flipped on the transistor radio he kept next to the sagging armchair in the living room and listened as the details of the double police murder filled the quiet, shabby room. The newscaster said the police suspected a rifle sniping, but Henry Cyrus wasn't mentioned. He turned the radio off, went back into the bedroom, and rummaged through his dresser drawer, where he found the faked identification he had used once before. He shoved it in an old wallet.

As he was about to leave, the phone rang. He debated picking it up, then on a hunch, grabbed it on the fourth ring.

"Joe, good to hear your voice." It was his ex-wife Eleanor. Her timing remained perfect. "I called the precinct, but they said you were on vacation. I found that hard to believe, since I don't ever remember you taking a single day off, but I suppose miracles sometimes happen. Is that girl with you?"

Jesus, Ryker thought, this was nuts. "Hello, Ellie," he said. "How's the jockstrap account?"

"Bulging," she said, laughing. "But I told you, it's pantyhose this time. The boys from North Carolina really have a sensational new product. We're going to blitz the test market next month and see just how well we can . . ."

He let her go on and on about her business and her friends, not interrupting, not really listening either. As quickly as he could, he got her off the phone, yet sometimes, he thought, she was his last remaining link to the safe, comfortable world he had once thought he wanted. No more. What he had to do today would disgust Ellie.

At eleven A.M., he boarded an Eastern flight to Tulsa. At three P.M., he rented a Hertz Ford at Tulsa Airport using the fake driver's license and a counterfeit credit card. At five P.M., he pressed the doorbell of 143 Harrow Street, in Coffeyville, Kansas.

A washed-out looking blond woman answered the door.

"Yes?"

"Miss Cyrus? Sergeant Ryker, New York City Police. May I come in?" He knew if she asked to see his badge, there would be some unpleasantness. He silently cursed Avery again.

"Why not?" She opened the door. "City cops, FBI, State Police, now New York City. Why not?" She looked tired, bored—as though she'd been through it many times before. She had. "Sit down, Sergeant. . . ."

"Ryker. Thank you."

"Cup of coffee?"

"Sure."

He sat in a stained armchair and looked around as she disappeared into the kitchen. A house with the husband, wife, or lover missing had a special look. This place looked like his own apartment, so he decided that she had once had a live-in lover, but he was gone. A low cry from the back of the house reminded him that she had a child. This was the deceased parents' house, he figured.

She returned with a cup of coffee and sat opposite him, across the coffee table. They looked each other over for a minute. Ryker put her age at about thirty-five. Almost pretty. Blue eyes—no life in them, though. Blond hair with a touch of red. She spoke first.

"What could you possibly want with me now? You have Henry. He's innocent," she said mechanically. "Why don't you let him go?"

"He used to call you—while we were looking for him."

"No. I saw him once in New York City, though."

"That's not true, Miss Cyrus. We have copies of the reverse charge calls from New York."

"So? He always called from a booth. I never knew where he was. Why are you bothering me with that now?"

"Well, you see, he's been released."

"By who?" She looked surprised.

"Friends of his. Anyway, we discovered we had a few more questions we forgot to ask him. We thought maybe he'd come back here." Ryker knew that there was no way Cyrus would chance coming back to Coffeyville. He'd probably passed a half dozen FBI men on the road driving here.

The woman looked suspicious. "Why should he? He has nothing here."

"Well, you're his sister. He has a niece." He nodded toward the back room. "He's fond of you. We know that from the telephone conversations."

"You—you tapped my phone?"

"Not us. The FBI."

"Get out of here."

"We thought perhaps he would call you again—I'm sure he will."

"Please leave, Mr.—"

"Sergeant Ryker. Well," he said, standing, "if he does call, give him a message for me, please."

The girl stood. "What is it?"

"This—" His fist shot out and buried itself in her soft belly. She doubled over and gasped for air. Ryker grabbed her by her long hair and straightened her up. Slowly, methodically, he slapped her with his big open hand, across her face and breasts. Her legs buckled and she sank to her knees. Ryker bent down and grabbed the front of her blouse with both hands. In one violent jerk, he ripped open the blouse and bra. Silent tears poured down her face. He knelt down and grabbed her hair again. He growled directly into her ear. "You tell Henry that Sergeant Joe Ryker was asking about him. You tell him that if he has any balls, he'll want to talk to me."

The woman shook her head violently. "No."

Ryker pulled on her hair harder. "I hear from the boys downtown that you give great blow jobs."

She turned and began clawing at his face.

Ryker thrust her forward on the floor and kicked her. "I'd like to stay around for one of your famous blow jobs, but I'm in a hurry. Here, take this, anyway." He pulled a quarter from his pocket and threw it on the floor in front of her face. "You make sure you tell Henry. Try not to forget, will you? Joe Ryker."

The woman lay quietly on the floor. Her body heaved with suppressed sobs.

Ryker walked to his car and got in. He was breathing hard, each breath reminding him of that scumbag Avery. His hands shook as he fished around in his pockets for the keys.

He still had a headache from the concussion grenade, and he chewed aspirins all the way back to Tulsa, got onto Interstate 44 and drove to the Oklahoma City Airport. He tried not to think about beating up the woman, but, of course, he could think of nothing else. It was a shithead thing to do, but Ryker had to admit it was his only shot at salvaging the case. What were a few black and blue marks compared to the damage Cyrus had already done? The end, he hoped, more than justified the means.

He forced himself to think about where Cyrus was at the moment. He wondered if he was still at large. He also wondered if he had left New York. Ryker was almost positive that Cyrus was still on the loose, and he had a strong hunch that the sniper would stay in the city, if only to exact more revenge against the police. A sane man would have been in Argentina by now, Ryker thought, but Henry Cyrus wasn't a sane man. Beating up his sister meant that Cyrus would stay in New York; meant that he didn't have to look for him anymore. Cyrus would find *him.* What he didn't know was if Barbara Cyrus would phone the police or not. It was a variable in his calculations, but it didn't matter that much. The worst that could happen would be that he'd be picked up before he reached the airport. He'd stand before some hayseed judge, deny everything, and walk out on low bail or no bail at all, after they confirmed that he was a cop. He'd be back in New York the next day at the latest. It wasn't the first time in his life that Joe Ryker knew what it felt like to be on the other end of the law. He smiled. Somehow he knew Barbara Cyrus wouldn't call the police. She belonged to that class of people who didn't trust or like policemen and Ryker certainly hadn't given her reason to change her mind.

A half hour after Ryker left Coffeyville, Barbara Cyrus was still on the floor sobbing. The ringing telephone brought her out of her stupor. She crawled the short distance to the kitchen phone, reached up and took down the receiver. Her brother's voice jarred her back to reality. She sobbed and cried into the mouthpiece for five minutes.

"Ryker?"

"Yes."

"New York Police?"

"Yes—Henry, what should I do?"

"Nothing—I'll take care of it." Cyrus thought hard. "Okay, just calm down. Reckon I'll just look up Mr. Ryker, as long as I'm in New York here."

"Henry—be careful. He's crazy."

"Don't you worry none. This feller ain't got no call to beat up my sister. I'll talk to him."

He replaced the receiver and stepped out of the phone booth. He looked around. The lobby of the huge, fifteen-hundred-room Sloane House Y.M.C.A. was bustling. He took an elevator and went directly to his room, lay down on the comfortable bed, and reviewed the events of the past twenty-four hours. After the shooting of the two policemen, he had run into a subway entrance in Harlem, bought a token, and boarded the first subway train that came along. It was the first time he had been in a subway, and the few other passengers stared at him curiously. A white man boarding the subway at One Hundred Tenth Street was odd enough, but a man who stood in the swaying car when so many seats were empty was weird. As he hung from the strap with one hand, he pressed on the long rifle under his coat with the other. The rifle was slipping down. The train had made a long stop at Times Square. After a few minutes, Cyrus had gotten off and begun walking south.

Later, standing in front of the massive building on West Thirty-fourth Street, he wondered if he weren't at the wrong address, but the sign definitely said "Y.M.C.A." Cyrus had once stayed in a "Y" in Lincoln, Nebraska, when he was eighteen, but this one looked as big and as frightening as the hotels that he wanted to avoid. The people, however, seemed extremely friendly.

He had signed himself in as Calvin Johnson, the name of a man he had once served with in the LRRP, and had paid in cash.

Now Cyrus pondered his next move. Last night's check-in had been easy, but he knew that his picture would soon be all over the place. An advantage of the cold, he realized, was that you could hide your face under a hat and scarf. Also, the gun was much easier to conceal under a big coat. Still, he didn't like the cold, and the parks were definitely out, as far as cover and concealment. The Y.M.C.A. was inexpensive for New York, but he knew he couldn't stay there.

He patted the long low bulge under the covers of his bed. "What do you think, Mikey? You ready to leave this here good old 'Y'? Damn, it sure was cold in that park—and you layin' in the ground like that, all froze up when I found you. Almost let me down when I needed you.

"Well, we got about four of them last night. Two for sure. Now we got to get at least one more before we go. Them cops think they're so damn smart."

Suddenly he thought about the phone call he had just made to his sister. "Damn, I musta been on ten minutes! Called from this here lobby, too. Shit! We gotta move, old buddy. Up and at 'em." Cyrus sprang from his bed, lashed the M-14 and scope to his side with a cord from the curtain, and put on his coat.

Outside, he walked quickly through the cold dark toward the Port Authority. He had noticed that the area was dotted with large military surplus stores, so he entered one on West Forty-second Street. The enormous warehouse-type outlet was just what he was looking for. He purchased boots, an oversized coat, gloves, a fur hat, thermal underwear, a ski mask, and some other items. There were no clerks to bother him, and as he walked to the check-out counter he noticed a sporting goods section. He was in desperate need of 7.62 mm rounds. He had recovered only one magazine of twenty rounds from his cache. He hesitated and wondered if they would have what he needed, then, reluctantly, he decided not to take the chance. After he had paid for his purchases, he left.

He crossed quickly to the Port Authority Bus Terminal, slipped into a pay toilet and changed, feeling as though he were starting a new life. On the wall among all the other graffiti, a man who knew what use was made of these pay toilets, had written, "Beware of all enterprises that require new clothes—Henry David Thoreau." Cyrus didn't see it and, if he had, wouldn't have cared. He had a job to do.

He left the large pay toilet and walked into the massive main lobby. He bought a *Daily News* from a vendor. On page three, he saw his own face staring back at him. He was not surprised. On the same page were the pictures of the two uniformed policemen he had killed the night before.

"Here we go again," was all he could think to say.

TWELVE

Peterson was distraught. The events of the last few days had completely unnerved him. Things seemed to be coming apart. He knew instinctively that he should never have fucked with Ryker, but he had had no choice at the time. Now as he stared at the faces around the long table, he had a feeling that he had been through all this before. He had. "Lindly, have you heard from ESU yet?"

"Yes, sir. They'll have ten anti-sniper teams on the roofs tonight—all in this area."

"How about Floyd Bennett Field?"

"Four choppers—weather permitting."

"Lieutenant, are all the exits to the city being watched?"

"Yes, sir," Fischetti said. "Do you think he'll stay or go?"

"Stay," Avery answered.

Peterson looked up. "Why?"

"Your boy Ryker just did a tap dance on Henry's sister."

"What! Ryker is in Coffeyville?"

"Not anymore. We had her phone tapped again after last night, and one of our agents saw a man matching Ryker's description enter and leave her house. Cyrus called her from the Y.M.C.A. on Thirty-fourth Street. Stayed on a little too long this time. We called the precinct down there, but the cops missed him by about five minutes. Used an alias of Calvin Johnson to check in."

"Son-of-a-bitch." Peterson felt as though he were living a nightmare. "What did Cyrus say to his sister? Where's Ryker? Why didn't you pick him up?"

Avery was trying to hide a little smirk. He seemed to find Peterson amusing this evening. "Well, Henry implied that he was going to blow Ryker away. That's why I think he'll stay. Secondly, Ryker must have used an alias, too. I don't think he flew directly back to New York either.

"Anyway, we couldn't pick up his trail. As far as pulling him in, he hasn't done anything we can prove."

Peterson put his head in his hands. The four detectives in the room had never seen him look so bad. That made them happy. The killing of the two policemen, however, made them angry. As far as they were concerned, cop killing was the only serious crime on the books. Everything else was routine bullshit. Peterson had better not fuck up this time.

"Don't worry about Ryker," Avery continued. "He'll surface. He has to if he wants to flush out Cyrus."

"What's Ryker's status, by the way?"

Peterson was deep in thought and didn't answer. Finally, Fischetti said, "Still on vacation, officially. Of course if we could talk to him, we'd cancel it damn quick."

"Where's his partner?"

"Back in Queens. He changed his vacation to sick leave. We couldn't argue much with that. I'm sure Ryker will try the same thing so that we can't get him back under our control."

"How is that TV guy, Rogers, involved in this, by the way?" Lindly asked. He was confused.

Peterson looked up. "That bastard. I'll hang him one of these days."

Avery looked nonchalant, almost bored.

Lindly's partner, Wilkinson, walked into the room. He had been talking to the detectives in Harlem where the two cops were murdered. He sat down and looked at the silent men. Finally, he decided to break the silence. "Hey, where's this prick gonna hide now that the nuts and berries are gone from the parks?"

Peterson decided to try to get the small meeting back on a normal track. "I don't know. If he gets to know the ins and outs of the city, though, he'll find a place. Don't forget, thirty thousand homeless make it through the winter every year. They sleep over warm subway gratings, in flop houses, they hide in large public buildings overnight, some ride the subways all day or just curl up in an alley on mild nights. He'll get the hang of it if he wants to stay around bad enough."

"He wants to stay around bad enough," Avery said. "He wants to put one between Ryker's running lights." He tapped the bridge of his nose with his finger. "The guy's got balls—you have to give him that much."

"Who?"

"Cyrus," Avery answered. "Ryker, too, though," he added, grudgingly.

"They're both fucking nuts," Lindly said. "It should be a good match."

Peterson stood. "There won't be any match, damn

it. I want Cyrus picked up as quickly as possible, and I want Ryker brought to me as soon as he shows his face."

At nine P.M. Ryker dialed Craig Rogers's Westchester home from a bar on Ninth Avenue.

"You double-crossing bastard," Rogers said. "You almost killed my man!"

"Take it easy, Craig. You'll bust one of your golden vocal cords."

"I should have known better. If I go to jail, I'm taking you with me, you prick," Rogers roared.

"Craig, Craig. I have no idea what you're talking about," Ryker said. "It's been a rough week—listen, you have to do me a favor."

"What! Are you crazy?"

"We have a chance to pull this out yet—calm down and listen. You could still have a story."

"I have to get to the city—I have an eleven o'clock show, remember."

"They won't miss you. Listen, pull out the very best picture you have of me and show it tonight. Also, you have to get my picture in the papers. Use some old copy in connection with the Cyrus case . . . say I'm back on the case."

"What for?" Rogers was more than a little suspicious of Ryker, but he couldn't resist the possibility of a good story. It might erase the black mark he had hanging over him.

Ryker told him about his encounter with Barbara Cyrus and outlined his plan briefly.

"You beat up his sister? Are you crazy? What if he kills you? He's already killed two cops. Where's my story if he kills you?"

Ryker never considered that Cyrus would get him.

He thought a moment. "That's your story. If he kills me, you can tell the whole story. Make me a hero, Craig."

"Very funny. It will make you—and me, too, for that matter—look like an asshole. A lot of your buddies think that already, by the way."

Ryker shifted uneasily in the small booth. "Look, there's a bigger story—"

"It concerns the FBI, doesn't it?"

"You're a foxy son-of-a-bitch. My partner Hayes has all the facts on it. I'll tell him to fill you in on the whole thing if old Henry nails me."

"How do I know he'll tell me?"

"I'll tell him to, damn it. Officially, he doesn't know a thing about it. He got it all from me. He won't be incriminated. If you're not game, I can always go to Stillwell at WBI. . . ."

"Okay, okay; I'll run your picture."

The two men ironed out the details. When Ryker was satisfied, Rogers added, "I hope the bastard nails you," and hung up abruptly.

Ryker smiled and dialed Hayes's number. After a few rings, a woman answered.

Ryker identified himself.

"He's sleeping," Hayes's wife said. "I won't disturb him. What the hell have you two been . . ." Suddenly, Hayes's voice was on the other end.

"Ryker! Jesus Christ, I thought—where are you?"

"In limbo. I have a long story for you." Ryker related most of what happened since he walked out of the hospital, then gave Hayes instructions regarding Craig Rogers.

"You're crazy. That bastard will get you," Hayes said.

"Look, I'm not out to get shot. I'm going to have

enough trouble just getting him to find me—but when he does, it will be on my terms. I'll call you if I need a hand with anything."

"You can't."

"Why not?"

"Well—Mary is having the phone disconnected for a while."

"What the hell for?"

"Well, our little problem with Cyrus in the park . . . it's not officially recognized but . . ."

"Get on with it."

"Unofficially, there are plenty of people who know something about it. Mostly cops. After those two cops got killed . . . well, you and I are not the most popular guys—especially with the uniformed types. I've been getting calls here. . . ."

"I see. Okay. Let me think. Do you remember our friend Maureen?"

After a pause, Hayes answered, "Yes."

"I can be reached there—or leave messages with the desk clerk."

"I see." Hayes's voice sounded very guarded. Ryker knew that his wife was either on another extension or was standing very close.

Hayes continued, after a pause. "You're not going back to your apartment, then?"

"Are you kidding? That block will be lousy with cops and Feds. I hope Cyrus has the good sense to stay away from it, too."

"How is he going to find you then?"

"Watch Rogers's eleven o'clock news." Ryker hung up and called Peterson. Peterson's voice sounded much like Rogers's had a few minutes before.

"Where the hell are you?" Peterson shouted.

"On vacation."

"Where the hell are you?" he repeated.

"Listen, Captain. We've all been tiptoeing around the law for a long time with this Cyrus business. It's about time we wound it up, don't you think?"

"Your vacation is cancelled—get over here right now."

"With all due respect to your exalted rank, fuck you."

Peterson was stunned. "I'll flop you for that—I'll have you cleaning toilets in the Police Academy. . . ."

"We're both under the gun, Captain. I have you by the nuts over the deal you and the P.C. made with the FBI. Well, he's leaving with the old administration, taking a nice job in private industry, at a nice fat salary.

"How would it look if the public knew that you, the Feds, and the P.C. were all in cahoots, rubber-rooming Cyrus instead of nailing the bastard to the wall? I can see the headlines now: Mass Murderer Enjoys Vacation in Federal Facility, While Public Continues to Shake in Its Boots."

"How did you spring Cyrus?" Peterson said, quickly changing the subject.

"Don't know what you're talking about, Captain," Ryker said. "I was walkin' along, and all of a sudden there he is, so I said to myself, Ryker, doesn't that look like someone you know?"

"Can it, Ryker," Peterson said. "I'll get you for this anyway."

"All I want is a week's sick leave," Ryker said.

"You *are* sick, Ryker."

"There."

"I hope he . . ."

Ryker hung up. He sat down and had a few double Jack Daniels. At about ten-thirty P.M., the prostitute,

Maureen Malloy, came in. She spotted Ryker and walked over.

"I came as soon as I got your message," she said, standing next to him.

"Sit down." Ryker hadn't seen her since September. Her hair had grown out a bit, and it was blond again. "Need a roommate for a week or so?"

"After you straightened out Floyd for me, I guess I owe you something."

"Still hooking?"

She looked down. "Sort of. Freelance, though. I work during the day as a waitress in one of the restaurants in the Coliseum. Lots of out-of-town men there. Turns out I don't need a pimp. Damn sure don't need Floyd. I turn maybe two tricks a week—need the extra money."

"For what? Coke? Junk? Speedballs?" Ryker knew from long experience not to trust an addict. They were unreliable.

"Just chipping—nothing heavy." She knew it wasn't worth lying. He would soon see the fresh tracks on her thigh. At least she hoped he would see her thigh.

"How much?"

"Couple times a week—at night, when I don't have a john."

"You'd better be using clean needles. I don't want to catch AIDS from you. If I get anything at all—clap, herpes, anything—you're dead, got it?"

"Sure," she said. "I'm clean. Real clean."

"Clean as a fucking toilet," he said. "But I got no choice. Come on, we're going to your shithole room."

As they walked, Ryker looked for a tail. He didn't spot one, but couldn't be sure. He flagged down a passing cab, and they rode part of the way, then took a subway for a few stops, then a bus. As they walked the last few blocks, the young prostitute spoke. "Are you in trouble?"

"Only bad girls get into trouble."

They walked in silence for the next few blocks. The girl had trouble keeping up the pace. After a while she ventured, breathlessly, "Don't you have any luggage, honey?"

"Cut the 'honey' shit."

She looked hurt.

At the Saxon Hotel, Ryker walked quickly across the lobby and into the waiting elevator. He wanted to avoid both the desk clerk and the punk security guard. They'd remember him.

In Maureen Malloy's room, he went directly to the small Sony she kept on the table by her bed. A pathetic plastic Christmas tree stood blinking feebly next to it. He shut off the tree and turned on the TV. It was 11:03 P.M., and Craig Rogers's tanned, sincere face filled the screen.

"Hey, that reminds me. That guy, Cyprus something, the sniper . . ."

"Shut up."

Rogers's face was blurry, and the voice was tinny.

"Fix that damned thing," Ryker snapped.

She quickly obeyed, thinking she had just signed on for a rough couple of weeks.

"Coffee."

"Yes, sir."

"Cut the 'sir' shit and don't make any noise."

Maureen quietly removed her coat and began making instant coffee on a hotplate. She wasn't much of a cook; the coffee tasted like watery rust.

At 11:25, Rogers was almost finished with the news.

"That motherfucker."

"Who?"

"Shut up."

Finally, a big picture of Ryker began to materialize behind the newscaster's head. It was the picture Rogers's photographer had taken of Ryker and Hayes at the first sniping incident on the FDR Drive. This time, however, Hayes had not been cut out of it.

"It's Artie!" Maureen squealed. "It's you and Artie."

"Shut up."

Rogers began speaking. "As you know, two of New York's finest were gunned down last night in Harlem near the northern edge of Central Park. The police have stated that the ballistics of one of the recovered bullets match the rifle used in the terrible sniping incidents of this past summer." He paused.

Ryker was angry that Hayes's picture was still on the screen. "That asshole—I said *my* picture."

Rogers continued, summing up the case as if he were Captain Peterson. Finally, he said, "Sergeant Joe Ryker, seen on the right in the picture behind me, has been reassigned to the case. Sergeant Ryker has just returned from Kansas where he spoke with the suspect's sister. On his left is his partner, Arthur Hayes. We spoke with Sergeant Ryker earlier today at Vilella's Funeral Home on West Ninety-fifth Street, where one of the slain patrolmen, Victor Montoya, will be reposing the rest of the week. The sergeant told us that he thought the suspect, Cyrus, had probably left town and that police all over the country had been alerted. He added that the suspect would not dare stay in the city."

Ryker snapped off the set.

At least Rogers got most of it right, he thought. If he could get the same story repeated in the newspapers for the next few days, there was a good chance Cyrus would see it and come for him. It wouldn't look too unusual for a cop to visit a slain patrolman's family at a funeral home.

"More coffee?"

"I want a bourbon."

"I don't keep bourbon."

"Buy some tomorrow. Get undressed."

The hooker took off her clothes and threw them on an armchair. She stood naked and looked at Ryker. "On the floor?"

"What?"

"I thought . . . last time . . . you . . ."

"Don't be an idiot. Get into bed."

She slid back the covers, then squealed, her large breasts swaying as her hands frantically beat at something under the sheets. A few roaches scurried for cover. She shuddered. "I hate those things."

"Bedsheets?" Ryker asked, undressing.

"I wish I could get out of here—move uptown . . ."

"Look, we're going to be roommates," Ryker interrupted. "I don't want to hear your whining about how life could be better. You'll live and die a hooker and a junkie, probably right here in this fleabag. Concentrate on good fucking, please."

The hooker fought back tears as she tumbled onto the bed. Ryker checked the door, turned out the lights and moved over to the bed. The girl's milky white skin was a kaleidoscope of colors from the neon signs outside the window. A green light kept blinking on and off across her face.

Like fucking a pinball machine, Ryker thought.

Cyrus knelt on his coat behind a huge steel pillar under the elevated West Side Highway at West Forty-seventh Street. At 12:30 A.M., the area was completely deserted on this cold November night—except for the two uniformed patrolmen who had just left their squad car. The two cops checked doors and alleyways, then began walking back toward their warm car—toward Cyrus.

Cyrus was shivering with the cold. He pressed the gun barrel against the steel pillar to keep the shaking gun stable while he considered for a moment. The targets were over four hundred yards away, but they were bouncing and hopping to keep warm as they walked. The exhaust from their car partly clouded their image. He was shaking, and the gun was shaking. He wished for a perch rather than a blind, because if he missed or wounded one or both of them, he was in trouble. They had a radio and guns. He became nostalgic for the good days of summertime hunting and considered passing up this chance opportunity and waiting for Ryker.

The cops separated as they came toward the car. One man walked on the sidewalk; the driver began walking in the street.

Cyrus was the type of hunter who couldn't pass up any target, no matter how dangerous it was. He remembered taking a shot at a big grizzly in the Ozark mountains once. He and his father had only single-shot shotguns. His was an old .410 Browning, and he had used a deer slug in place of the shotgun shell. He wounded the grizzly, and the bear had chased him and his father for the better part of an hour. After they'd made it back to their pickup truck, his father had beat the hell out of him. "You take a fool's shot like that again when my back's turned, I'll stake you out and leave you for the grizzlies." Henry had not learned his lesson. He had been the same kind of sniper in

Vietnam. No one wanted to go on patrol with him; that's why he had volunteered as an LRRP. He worked alone.

He remembered all this as he stared through the scope at their icy blue images. The two cops had stopped and were staring back at him. He knew they couldn't see him at four hundred yards in the dark, but he used it as an excuse to make his decision. He had lots of excuses to shoot.

"Reckon they see us, Mikey. What the hell, can't dance, too wet to plow, might as well shoot."

He chose the one on the right, the one on the sidewalk, using the cop's silver badge as an aiming point. He wanted both targets in his scope at the same time, but he had to make do with what came his way.

He squeezed the trigger. The silent report made the gun clang loudly against the cold steel pillar. He swung the gun to the left before he could see if his first round had found its mark. He moved the gun frantically but could not find the second cop in his scope. Instinctively, he swang back to his first target. The cop was still standing and had his back to him now. He was looking at the building. Cyrus concluded that the round had missed and buried itself in something, making a noise. It couldn't have ricocheted. He knew they would have recognized *that* sound and would have been jumping all over one another to find cover. Now the second cop came into the scope. Both men drew their guns and crouched with their backs toward him.

"Once more," Cyrus said, as he squeezed the trigger again. The gun jumped. He moved it slightly and sent another round down range, watching as both cops pitched forward and lay side by side on the cold sidewalk.

He rose stiffly, broke down the weapon and lashed the pieces to his body with heavy surgical tape. He shrugged on the huge coat and moved quickly toward Times Square. It was the only part of the city he knew where there would still be plenty of people on the street.

In eleven minutes, he was in front of an obscure porno movie theater on West Forty-fourth Street. He went inside. Even though the place smelled of urine and semen, he luxuriated in the warmth. He ran his hand over his slow-growing beard and decided it wouldn't look right for weeks. Still, he looked better than most of the patrons in the theater. Cyrus disapproved of pornography, so he dozed off.

At two-fifteen, he felt a hand on his shoulder. He jumped up with a start and began to draw his big army Colt .45 from his coat pocket.

"Get out. This ain't no all-night theater," a big black woman snarled. She pronounced "theater" as if it had three syllables.

"Get on out, motherfucker," she said, prodding him.

Cyrus opened his hand, and the heavy gun dropped to the bottom of his deep pocket. He looked around and blinked. The house lights were on, and the theater was even more disgusting than he had imagined. No one had bothered to clean it for a week. He could smell rats.

Cyrus pulled his hat down over his eyes, slid past the woman, and walked outside. He cursed himself for falling asleep. Times Square was still alive with crack and cocaine dealers, druggies from New Jersey, homosexuals from Connecticut, pimps, prostitutes, late diners and winos. It would stay this way until dawn drove them back to whatever holes they had come out of. It seemed to Cyrus that there was an unusually large number of cops around, so he walked and poked around for the next hour, even chancing a hot cup of coffee. Eventually, he fell in with a group of derelicts looking for a place to crash. He joined them as they found refuge for the remainder of the night in a heated parking garage. The attendant collected a dollar from each of them and led them to a fleet of trucks that were in for the night. They each made themselves comfortable on the luxury of the padded front seats. Cyrus had some misgivings. The multi-storied garage was a dead end with only one entrance and exit; he slept uneasily.

At first light, the parking attendant honked on one of the truck horns and rousted the sleeping derelicts. Cyrus jumped down from the truck cab, running in place and slapping his arms together until the circulation began returning to his numb limbs. He could see his breath as he exercised and wondered why they advertised this place as a heated garage. Walking quickly from the garage, he separated himself from the derelicts and headed east on Forty-second Street. Near Broadway, he stopped at Hotalings newsstand. He was confused looking at the more than four hundred different newspapers displayed: Chinese, Hebrew, Arabic and Russian characters mystified him. He moved down the counter until he found a section with familiar lettering. He searched in vain for something in English.

"Help you, Mac?"

Cyrus looked up. "Uh, *Daily News?*"

"Which one? Hamilton, Brisbane, London?"

"Uh, New York."

The newsdealer pulled a morning edition from under the counter and laid it on top. "Thirty-five cents, bud."

Cyrus fumbled in his pocket around the Colt .45, found thirty-five cents, and paid for the paper.

As he walked along, he looked up at the moving ribbon of news as it traveled around the former Times Tower building. Henry Cyrus hoped he would see his name in lights today, as he had a few times during the past summer. He also became aware that no one else was watching the running ribbon. He became uneasy and moved on before he attracted any attention.

He bought a variety of candy bars from a small store, then looked for a place to eat them and read his paper. Standing around in this blustery cold might be conspicuous, so Cyrus considered going back to the cavernous Port Authority Bus Terminal, but he figured correctly that it would be one of the most watched places in the city this morning.

Rush hour traffic was becoming heavier, and the sidewalks were crowded. The boy from Coffeyville, Kansas, wondered again where all these people came from. The biggest city he had ever been in before he came to New York was Saigon. He had felt as strange there as he did here. Cyrus was tired, and he knew he had a full day of walking and wandering ahead of him. He also realized that he could walk the streets much more freely in winter all bundled up than he ever could in summer, so he decided to take advantage of his cover and explore the city. He turned into the rising sun along Fiftieth Street, which looked busy. He remembered vaguely that someone had once told him there were lots of girls on the east side. It wasn't girls he was looking for, though, but an answer to his problem of how to deal with Ryker. Along the way, he ate a few of the candy bars, wondering if he should talk to the rifle strapped to his body as he walked. It was never clear in his disturbed mind whether or not the rifle could hear him when it was broken down into its component parts.

"Mikey—you listening, Mikey?" He spoke softly as he walked. "This Ryker: how we gonna find him, old buddy? We don't know where he lives. How do we find him?"

He had the answer to that question tucked under his arm. On page five of the *Daily News,* Rogers's nonexistent interview with Ryker appeared next to the picture of Ryker and Hayes. The paper had promised Rogers they would plant a story or a paragraph every day about Ryker's daily visits to the funeral home on West Ninety-fifth Street.

As Cyrus walked east, he could see that this area of the city was less commercial and more wealthy than the west side. A few well-dressed people walked on Park Avenue, but the crowd was too thin here, he thought, feeling conspicuous in his shoddy clothes. Cyrus turned abruptly and began the walk back. At Sixth Avenue he turned left, vaguely remembering that there was a small park here somewhere. At Forty-second Street, he found it. Bryant Park was located directly behind the Public Library. For some reason, the park was elevated about five feet above street level. This looked promising. Cyrus climbed the stairs behind a newsdealer's stand and looked around. There were enough bums, dealers, hookers, and pigeon feeders sitting in the cold sunshine to make him feel safe.

He sat on a bench and unwrapped the last of his candy bars. While he ate, he anxiously scanned the paper for a story about last night's police killings, but the murders had happened too late to make the early edition. He found the plant, however, and read, "Sergeant Joe Ryker made the statement while coming from Vilella's Funeral Home on West Ninety-fifth Street, where he had been paying his respects to the family of the slain patrolman. He said he planned a three-day vigil."

The killer laid the paper beside him and smiled as he threw a few peanuts from a Baby Ruth bar to the pigeons.

THIRTEEN

Ryker had been sitting in a pew at the funeral home since it had opened at nine. Every fifteen minutes he would get up, walk through the depressing building, stand on the front steps, take a few drags on his cigar, snuff it out, drop it back in his pocket, and go back inside.

He now sat on the uncomfortable pew and looked at his watch. Twelve-fifteen P.M. He felt the thin .25 Beretta automatic in his pocket. It didn't make him feel secure.

He waved to the passing funeral director, a swarthy Hispanic man wearing a gray pinstripe suit and a look of professional concern. Ryker noticed that all funeral directors looked alike, regardless of race or nationality. If death was the great equalizer, then the embalming business ran a close second, he thought.

Ryker got up again and began pacing back and forth in the overheated, empty—almost empty, he was with the corpse—chapel.

The piped-in organ music was giving him a headache; bored, he walked over to the coffin and looked down into the open casket. The young cop, Montoya, had been shot in the head, but the cosmeticians had done a near perfect job of restoration. He could see a heavy caking of makeup on the left temple. *That must be where the bullet entered,* he thought idly, going over his plan one more time.

The whole idea was to get back to the Saxon Hotel before the sun set. He didn't relish the idea of being on the street after dark with Cyrus on the loose; bravery was one thing, stupidity, another. He would have to keep track of the time. There were no windows in the chapel. His most dangerous exposure was entering and leaving the building, but that was a calculated risk he felt he had to take.

The funeral director walked up to him, but Ryker was so deep in thought, he hadn't heard the man. *Funeral directors walk as quietly as the dead,* he told himself. With any luck, he would at least be able to hear the large outside door open, if Cyrus came in.

The funeral director, whose name was Angelada, said, "A terrible tragedy. Such a fine young policeman."

"Part of the job."

"Perhaps. But for what reason? Were the others friends of yours, too?"

"What others?"

The funeral director looked surprised. "Last night. Certainly you heard . . ."

Ryker began tearing through the newspaper.

"No. No. It happened very late," Angelada said. "It is not in this paper, but it's been on the radio—all morning."

Ryker jumped up. "Where's the radio?"

"Here, follow me."

The funeral director led Ryker into his office.

Ryker switched to an all news channel and waited for the story to be repeated. He listened as the newscaster gave the details: both cops had lived in New Jersey; funeral services were to be held in their respective hometowns.

Too far for Henry, Ryker thought. It's going to have to be here.

The funeral director put on his professionally sad face. "They were friends, also?"

"Almost. Wrong hometown," Ryker said, walking out of the office.

He went outside and lit a fresh cigar, thinking about telling the funeral director to keep an eye out for Cyrus.

Too risky, he decided. The man would blow it if he knew. Probably go all shifty-eyed and scared the minute Cyrus opened his mouth to ask him something. No. It had to look like just what it seemed to be—a friend mounting a long vigil for a slain comrade-in-arms.

Ryker looked up and down the quiet street. If he were being watched by the law, they must be using a rotating stake out, he thought. He couldn't pick out anyone he had seen on his past cigar breaks. He threw the butt away and went back inside.

Peterson sat alone in his office at One Police Plaza, the *Daily News* spread out on his desk. He rested his head in his hands, struggling with his dilemma. Ryker had made himself perfectly clear when he said, "Keep away from me." But now he had a chance to nail Cyrus by following Ryker—if he could get the manpower. They would have to be people Ryker wouldn't recognize, so that limited him. A few months ago he could have called the Police Commissioner or Chief of Detectives. But his friends and rabbis in the department were treating him as if he had leprosy—or worse, AIDS. When he had called the outgoing Police Commissioner's office, the secretary had said, "The commissioner is too busy transferring his duties to the new P.C. to come to the phone, Captain." Vainly, Peterson had left a carefully worded message and hung up. That was over two hours ago. Ryker had been right. He, Peterson, was left holding the old scumbag.

Even Chief of Detectives McVey, who had always bent over backwards to help Peterson, was suddenly "in conference," and a personal appearance by Peterson in his office brought only downcast looks from the Chief's secretary and silence from behind the Chief's door. With the outgoing P.C., McVey's chances of remaining Chief of Detectives were nil.

There had to be someone he could trust, he thought, someone who could do his dirty work for him. He was fighting for his career and he knew it. It was frightening.

Most frightening of all, though, was that Avery had not returned his calls either. Suddenly he felt very alone. He wondered if this would be a good time to go on vacation. He considered calling the FBI office again, but he didn't want to appear too panicky.

Finally, at one P.M., as Peterson was considering going home for the day, Avery called. Peterson gripped the phone. "Where the hell have you been?"

"I'm not on your payroll, Captain. It's my business where I've been."

Peterson had a feeling that the last rat was leaving the sinking ship. "Look," he said in the calmest voice he could muster. "Today's *Daily News* has a story . . ."

"I know. I saw it this morning."

Peterson waited for more, but there was only silence. He wanted to say, "Then why the hell didn't *you* call *me?"* Instead, he said, "What are we going to do about it?"

"We? When did *we* form a corporation? What are *you* going to do about it? You should have that funeral home covered. Throw a couple of men in the caskets if you have to. There's at least a fifty-fifty chance Cyrus will show if he saw that plant and fell for it. Why do I have to explain your job to you?"

Peterson fought to keep his temper under control. Picking and choosing the words carefully, he told Avery about Ryker's threat. Also, speaking in guarded terms, he told Avery that the Police Commissioner hadn't returned his call.

Avery listened without commenting as Peterson spoke. When the desperate-sounding voice on the other end stopped, he said, "You feel all alone?"

Peterson didn't answer.

"Look, Captain, you know damn well we can't help you. If worse comes to worst, arrest Ryker and charge him with something."

"Have you got any evidence he sprang Cyrus?"

"Not that you'll ever get."

Peterson was getting angrier. "If we make the collar on Ryker, he'll spill his guts. If we collar Cyrus and he has that damned rifle with him, we're going all the way with murder one. The only way you'll get him is after he's spent forty or fifty years in a state prison."

"You have to go with murder one and go for a conviction anyway."

"What? Why?"

"Why? All those goodies in Cyrus's hole—grenades, seven-point-six-two millimeter ammo, plastic explosives. His prints are all over that stuff. It's enough to make a case even without the gun."

"You have that stuff—it's your goddamned property—you said you would bury it."

"We don't want to bury it anymore. There won't be a Federal conspiracy trial after all."

"Why not?"

"We don't care much anymore."

"What?"

"Well." Avery paused. "I've been meaning to tell you: We've got pretty much all of the gun running ring nailed down, to tell you the truth. We're going to start making arrests in January. Cyrus was only a customer, it turns out. He doesn't know anything. We don't need him. The evidence from the hole was turned over to your Property Division, by the way. I had it sent over this morning. The D.A. was notified."

Peterson was stunned. "You bastard. We have four cops dead."

"Your boy Ryker and that idiot Rogers got him turned loose."

"Only because you didn't want that murdering bastard busted for murder, you son-of-a-bitch."

"It seemed like a good idea at the time, but the best laid plans of mice and men . . ."

"I don't believe this."

"Look, now that we don't need him and he has his toy and he's stalking Ryker, it seems that your job is pretty clear. I'm going back to Washington. There is no one else here who knows about this case—do you understand? If you recover our rifle and scope, call us. It's been a real pleasure working with New York's finest, Captain. Good luck and Happy Thanksgiving."

The phone went dead, and Peterson stared stupidly at it.

Hayes paced up and down the living room of his Queens home. For the fifth time that day, he was listening to the radio accounts of the slaying of the last two patrolmen.

"It's my fault," he kept repeating. "It's all my fault."

His wife looked worried. "It's not your fault, honey. It's that sergeant of yours . . ."

"No. It's really their fault. The Commissioner, Peterson, the FBI."

"The FBI?"

Hayes had given his wife only the barest facts of the case. She didn't seem to comprehend any of it; Hayes had to admit that he didn't fully understand it himself.

"What difference does it make? Four cops dead, and they blame Joe and me."

As the story of Hayes's part in the release of Cyrus traveled through the blue grapevine of the police department, he knew their hostility would get much worse. Of course, the uniformed cops knew that there must have been a motive of some sort, but they also knew that somehow Ryker and Hayes had failed, and suddenly blue uniforms and not blond hair had become the target of death.

"They don't even know I'm on sick leave. Nobody knows the story. It's all rumors and locker-room bullshit," Hayes said, grinding his hands together.

"Sit down, honey. The doctor said . . ."

"I want you and the kids out of here. Go back to Montauk. Stay with your mother. Start packing now."

"No. I'm staying with you."

Hayes realized that she meant it, so he said, "I'm worried about the kids. Take them out to Montauk, then you can come right back."

An hour later, a taxi pulled up in front of the house. The driver honked. Mary Hayes and the two children kissed Arthur Hayes good-bye and entered a cab bound for Penn Station in Manhattan.

The young cop walked back into his house, stood alone in the middle of his living room for a moment, then walked upstairs. He took a bottle of bourbon from his dresser, sat on his bed and began drinking from the bottle. He drank and brooded for an hour or so. Finally he got off the bed and opened the bedroom closet, pulled out his old patrolman's uniform, dusted it off and put it on.

An hour later, he walked up the steps of the IRT subway station at Columbus Circle and Fifty-ninth Street. He had no clear plan in his mind, but felt like walking a beat as an ordinary patrolman. It was five o'clock and already dark.

Ryker was restless. He had read the *Post* from cover to cover, including the full account of the last double police slaying under the West Side Highway. He also noticed that the story about him "visiting frequently at the funeral home on West Ninety-fifth Street" was attached to the shooting story. The *Post* also carried a small picture of him. He realized that Rogers had a lot of pull in this town.

Several cops had come in briefly during the day. Some came to see Montoya, but some had seen the story in the newspapers and came to stand and glare at Ryker. Not one of the uniformed cops said a word to him.

Ryker thought, *At least someone is being pulled in*

by my newspaper ad. I hope the next son-of-a-bitch who walks through the door is Cyrus.

He glanced at his watch and noted that it was already five-thirty. It was dark outside. He rose to leave. Suddenly, there was a lot of noise in the foyer. Ryker spun around. A group of at least fifteen of Montoya's relatives were coming into the chapel. They all wore black; they were all crying. The funeral director was speaking in Spanish and pointing toward Ryker.

"Oh, fuck," Ryker said quietly.

Then a dozen people were all over him, pawing at him, speaking rapidly in Spanish and crying. Ryker didn't like displays of emotion, and all the touching was making him uneasy. He wanted to get away, but he knew that he had to play the game.

Finally one of the older men who spoke English said, "We know you must go back to work to catch the murderer of Victor—but his parents request that you pray with them at the casket."

"I'm Jewish," Ryker lied.

After some more talk in Spanish, the man turned to Ryker and smiled, "*Señor* and *Señora* Montoya say it would be an honor to kneel with you and pray side by side—they to Jesus, you to Moses.

"They also tell me to say that no matter what they have heard, they know you are not responsible for Victor's death. Would a guilty man keep such a vigil?"

Ryker was guilty and exasperated but could see no way out of it. He walked to the casket, and for the first time since he was a child, he knelt with his hands clasped in front of him. He did not pray.

Outside the funeral home, Henry Cyrus looked up and down the block. He was not unaware that the story in the papers might be a trap. Consequently, he had left his rifle hidden in nearby Riverside Park. He wanted to kill Ryker more than anything else in the whole world right now. The most important thing for the moment was a reconnaissance of the terrain. He had learned that much in the army.

Half expecting to be surrounded by cops at any moment, he began walking again toward the funeral home. When he was in front of it, he mounted the steps quickly and went inside. In the lobby, he saw a sign with an arrow that said "Montoya."

His heart was beating rapidly as he walked down the narrow hall. When he reached the inner foyer, he peered into the chapel. A hand grasped him by the shoulder from behind. Cyrus spun around. The light-footed funeral director, Angelada, smiled.

"You are a friend of Victor's? A policeman?" The undertaker knew this *anglo* couldn't be a relative.

"Uh, is Joe Ryker here?"

"At the casket. You see him? He is praying."

Cyrus looked around. He could see the large back about thirty feet from him. His hand tightened around the Colt .45 in his pocket.

"Is he staying—long?"

"He will not be long—he must leave. He has the night duty."

"I can't wait—will he be back tomorrow?"

"Every day until the funeral. He was a great friend of Victor's. Did you know Victor?"

"No. Just met him once," Cyrus said. He turned and walked rapidly out of the funeral home, down the dark street and headed toward Riverside Park. No one stopped him. He was convinced now that he wasn't being set up. Ryker was praying at the coffin. The funeral guy seemed straight. It was going to be all right. His finely tuned instincts weren't sending him any danger signals . . . yet something was wrong.

"He has the night duty," he said to himself. If he couldn't locate Ryker later at night, it would have to be a day job. Cyrus didn't like that—he didn't like it at all. *Maybe the time to do it was right now,* he thought. *Right here and now.* The killer looked up at the surrounding buildings. Decision time again.

FOURTEEN

Peterson had finally come to a decision. The more he thought about it, the more sense it made. He wanted two things, he realized. First, he wanted Henry Cyrus captured, charged with murder and convicted, or he wanted him dead. Like every cop, no matter how much lip service he paid to "due process," he would rather see a known killer shot down on the streets like a dog than see him go before a jury.

The other thing he wanted, no matter how much he tried to put it out of his mind, was Ryker. Dead. Ryker, who threatened to rock the boat—to blow the whistle on a secret deal. He thought about his job. His home. His two daughters in college. His wife. There was no way around it. The worst he could be accused of would be bad judgment. Bad judgment for not saturating the area around the funeral home with plainclothes cops. Bad judgment for not getting some anti-sniper teams in the area. Simply bad judgment. A letter of reprimand from the P.C., maybe. At least no one would accuse him of murder.

In short, Carl Peterson, Captain, N.Y.P.D., faced with the fact that a known killer might be in a certain area at a certain time and that one of his men was in imminent danger of being killed and that he could prevent the killing and arrest the killer, did nothing. He went home.

In his office on the second floor of the Eighth Precinct, Lieutenant Fischetti toyed with the slips of paper on his desk. They were two phone messages, both from Peterson. He wondered what to do. If he kept his mouth shut about Peterson's deal with the Feds, maybe everything would blow over. If he made a stink, they'd flop him and send him back to Staten Island where he had languished for years. He tried to tell himself that he wasn't really a part of the conspiracy, having found out about it by accident. He thought the whole thing stank worse than an old hooker's snatch, but he also liked being a lieutenant in Manhattan. He wondered what to do.

Fischetti walked out of his small office cubicle and sat on Lindly's desk. "Do you think Peterson saw this?" he said, holding a copy of the *News*.

"I know he saw it this morning. I pointed it out to him myself, over at the House of Brass," he said, referring to One Police Plaza.

"Maybe he's done something already."

"What would he do without telling you?"

"I don't know—something is being done at some level, I'm sure," Fischetti said, thinking maybe the two phone messages on his desk were about this.

"Bullshit. This whole thing sucks. First Cyrus escapes. Hayes and Ryker wind up in the hospital—nobody seems to know how, Cyrus blows away two cops, Ryker beats the shit out of Cyrus's sister, the media fall all over themselves giving out the address of Vilella's Funeral Home, where Ryker is sitting with the bereaved family. Shit, it's an obvious plant that didn't come out of *this* office. And as far as we know, nobody is watching Joe—except maybe Cyrus."

Fischetti stood. "I don't know. What can I do by myself? Maybe it's all taken care of. I don't want to foul any plans somebody higher made."

"Nobody made any plans to cover Ryker, damn it. If they did, you would know about it—can't you understand that?"

"Maybe he doesn't want to be covered. Maybe he wants to go it alone."

"What the hell difference does that make? This is the police force, not a Rambo flick. We don't have any loners here. Get on the stick, Lieutenant."

Fischetti began pacing. He stopped and looked at Lindly. "How many anti-sniper teams did you get from ESU?"

"Ten teams of two men each," he said.

"Are they in position yet?"

Lindly looked down at his watch. "Six P.M. A few of them are. Some will come on later. They all have radios anyway."

"How is the command structure set up? Can we divert them?"

"Sure. My liaison is a Sergeant Moriarity. I can call him and tell him we have a lead. How many do you want?"

"Two—no, better make it one team. We don't want to make a big thing out of it. Too many questions to answer. Get them on the West Park Houses. Those are the tallest buildings around the funeral home, I guess. They should be able to see most rooftops in the area. How about the choppers?"

"They go that route anyway."

"Call them and tell them we may have a tip. Ask

them to keep a special eye out in the West Nineties. No excessive hovering though."

"Okay, good. How about some bodies down in the street?"

Fischetti pondered. He didn't like to make so many decisions all at once. It gave him a headache. "No, just call downstairs and make the patrol cars in the area aware that we have a possible lead. Nothing more."

"Okay, if that's the way you want it. How about during the day—tomorrow, if nothing happens tonight?"

"We'll worry about it tomorrow. Anyway, Cyrus probably won't make a move during the day. Make those calls. I'm going home. I have to rest up for all the explaining I'll have to do tomorrow."

"You don't have to explain shit to anybody."

"Wanna bet?"

Fischetti left, and Lindly called ESU and asked that an anti-sniper team be put on the West Park Houses. He also asked for a second team to be placed somewhere on Ninety-fifth Street around Vilella's Funeral Home.

Cyrus had made his decision. He didn't want to go for Ryker during the day. He wanted him at night, and he wanted him in the cross hairs of his Mark V scope.

He had walked back to Riverside Park, retrieved the rifle from the branches of an evergreen tree, and hurried back to Ninety-fifth Street. He needed a perch or a blind to shoot from and he needed it soon. The residential area was made up of three- to five-story walk-up apartments. Some of them, like the funeral home, were converted brownstone townhouses. Cyrus kept looking. The area didn't seem too promising. He wondered if Ryker had left yet.

There were few pedestrians and little street traffic.

Cyrus considered just kneeling at the head of the block where he stood and shooting if and when Ryker appeared.

Suddenly, the door of the funeral home swung open. A large figure took a few tentative steps down the stone stoop. Cyrus stepped into the shadow of a doorway. The figure on the steps looked up and down the block.

Ryker had finally broken away from the bereaved family. He left the funeral home and was now standing on the front stoop. He looked up and down the nearly deserted block. He knew he would have to walk east or west to an avenue to get away. He looked at his watch. Six-fifteen P.M.

Cyrus unbuttoned his bulky coat and swung the already assembled rifle up and out and peered through the scope for a second. He put the rifle back in his coat. He had no doubt that the face in the scope was Joe Ryker. He raised the rifle again and aimed. The target was one hundred yards distant and stationary. It was an easy shot. A very easy shot.

After walking his self-imposed beat for about an hour, Hayes went into a bar. He slipped into a phone booth and called the Saxon Hotel. The clerk rang Maureen Malloy's room and, after a few rings, she picked up the phone.

"Hello, Maureen? This is—"

"Artie!" She seemed genuinely happy to hear his voice.

"Yeah." He didn't know what to say. Finally, he decided that he'd better keep it on a business basis—his business, not hers. "Look, is Joe there?"

She seemed disappointed. "No. No, he's not. He

said he would be back before I got home and that I should leave my key at the desk. I bought bourbon and something for dinner. Do you think something happened . . . ?"

"No. Listen, I'll see you later. I'm in the city. The three of us can have a couple of drinks later. Like old times."

"Okay, honey. If he gets back I'll tell him."

"Right. Ask him to stay put until I get there."

"Okay."

"See you later."

Hayes hung up and looked down at his blue uniform. He was almost sober now, and suddenly he felt very foolish. He couldn't explain to himself why he put the uniform on or what it was he intended to prove. Maybe he hoped some of the uniformed cops on duty would see him. Still, he felt dumb. He didn't have to prove anything to anybody, he told himself. He considered going home, then thought, *what the hell, I'm here anyway.* He dialed Vilella's Funeral Home.

Very easy shot. Squeeze slowly.

Ryker suddenly turned, and in one quick motion mounted the steps of the funeral home and slid through the heavy oak door. He stood with his back to the door for several seconds. Sweat was forming on his brow. He had seen nothing and heard nothing, but something, the thing that had kept him alive all these years, told him to get inside that door and stay there. He wondered if he were losing his nerve or if his extra sense was particularly keen tonight. It might be a little bit of both, he decided.

After a few seconds, he turned toward the door again. A perverse instinct took hold of him. He was like a man who is afraid of heights and leans over the edge of the precipice, or a man who is afraid of water and runs into the surf and out again repeatedly. Like a man with a perverse tendency to dare and tempt his phobias, Ryker began to open the door. He wanted to get this thing over with, once and for all.

"Sergeant Ryker. Sergeant Ryker."

"What?" he said, with his hand on the brass doorknob.

"Telephone. Officer Hayes," Angelada said.

Ryker turned and followed the funeral director into his office. He noticed that his hand was shaking as he put the phone to his ear.

Cyrus lowered the rifle and slunk back into the doorway alcove.

"Son of a bitch. At least we know he's still there, Mikey. Gives us a little time to get a nice perch, don't it? We know there ain't no cops around here for sure now, anyway. Wonder why he went back inside so quick like. Do you reckon he can smell trouble like we can, old buddy?"

Cyrus walked onto the sidewalk and looked around again. Some of the nicer buildings had doormen. All of them looked occupied. He tried a few doorknobs. All of them were locked. He knew he could wait until someone came in or out of a door, but that would depend on the right positioning. New Yorkers, he knew, were a suspicious bunch. If he suddenly darted across the street and down the block and caught an opening or closing door, he would attract attention. If only there were a public building on the block. . . . "Funeral home! Damn right."

He hugged the long rifle to his side with one hand and thrust his other hand into his pistol pocket. Cyrus bolted across the street and shouldered the heavy door open. The small lobby was empty.

The funeral home was a converted brownstone that had been a private townhouse at one time. The stairs were right in front of him. A sign with the names Quevedo and Jimenez pointed up the stairs. Cyrus didn't know what these words meant, but it didn't matter. He mounted the creaking stairs three and four at a time. On the second floor he stopped. This floor held another large room. A few mourners from the Quevedo family stood and smoked in the hallway. One of them, a middle-aged man, looked at the killer as he stood, uncertainly.

"Jimenez," said the man, finally, as he pointed directly upward.

Cyrus smiled and nodded. He mounted the final stairway slowly and as nonchalantly as possible. On the third floor, he was confronted by the same scene.

"Quevedo," said an older woman as she pointed downward.

Cyrus walked past and headed for the roof stairs.

"Montoya?" the woman asked as she watched Cyrus.

Cyrus turned the corners around the stairwell. "Roof," he said as he smiled back at the mourners, as though he had some business there. He had.

He thanked his luck that there was no one from the funeral home on the third floor and that the last flight had been stairs and not a ladder hidden somewhere else. Cyrus had become an expert on New York rooftops. He climbed the stairs slowly and deliberately.

Ryker sat in the funeral director's office and pondered his next move. Hayes had insisted on coming to the funeral home. Ryker was against it, but when he learned that Hayes was packing a .357 Ruger Magnum in addition to his service revolver, he agreed. He decided to call a cab when Hayes arrived. He figured it would take him and Hayes less than three seconds to get into the cab and less than five seconds for the cab to make the turn onto West End Avenue. Cyrus, if he were waiting, couldn't be sure of his targets in that short amount of time. He would have to be constantly looking through the scope, and Ryker didn't think he would leave the scope on that long and chance running down the batteries. He sat and waited for Hayes. It was six-thirty.

For some unknown reason, Ryker found himself dialing his ex-wife's number in Chicago.

An unrecognizable woman's voice answered, "Ryker residence."

Joe Ryker was taken aback for a moment. Why had she kept the name she never wanted? "This is Mr. Ryker. Is Eleanor there?" He could hear music and voices in the background.

"Hold on," the woman said in a curt tone.

Ryker held the line, considered hanging up, almost did but held on. "Hello, Ellie, this is Joe. I love you. I'm quitting the job and coming to Chicago. Okay?" That was easy to say, he thought, but he couldn't say it to her. He held, listening to the music in the background.

Her voice came on the line. "Joe? Is anything wrong?"

"No. What's all that noise?"

"Cocktails. Come on up."

"The subway doesn't go that far."

"Well, what's up? You sound low."

"I'm in a funeral home. Low kind of place."

"A cop?"

"Yes."

"One of the ones the sniper shot?"

"Yes."

"I've been following it closely."

"Me, too."

"You're going to get killed one day, Joe."

"I know."

Neither spoke for some time, then Ellie said, "Do you want to talk?"

"No. Just wanted to . . ."

"Hear my voice? Say hello? Say good-bye?"

"Right."

"Stay alive. For God's sake, stay alive."

"I do my best."

"Call me at work tomorrow. Well . . . I'll be out most of the day . . . call me . . . let's see . . ."

Ryker smiled. "'Bye, Ellie. Thanks."

She hesitated, then said, "'Bye, Joe."

Ryker hung up.

The funeral director kept reminding himself to tell Ryker that another *anglo* had been looking for him earlier. The funeral business was so hectic at night though, he doubted he would find the time.

Cyrus knelt behind the brownstone parapet and looked down at the stone steps directly below him. He considered taking the scope off the rifle. At this distance, he would be too close to use it effectively. The picture in the scope would be blurry, and he had only a fourteen-degree field of view. At the thirty- or forty-foot distance Ryker would be from him as he left the funeral home, fourteen degrees would only give him a five- or six-foot wide picture in the scope. With the scope dismounted, he would be much better prepared at this short distance. The street lights would provide all the illumination he would need.

On the other hand, Ryker had to walk east or west

down the block. If he killed him as far away from the funeral home as possible, it would make his chances of escape that much better.

As he wrestled with his tactical problem, he turned on the scope and began scanning the nearby buildings and rooftops as a precaution. As he scanned toward West End Avenue he saw something that froze his blood more than the icy wind coming down the Hudson ever could. His heart literally skipped a beat. Across the street, on a rooftop two hundred yards away, were two men with the unmistakable silhouette of scopes mounted on long rifles. Cyrus threw himself down on the rooftop, behind the parapet and began shaking. Suddenly he was back in the jungle. He remembered laughing at the North Vietnamese anti-sniper teams with their Stone Age infrared equipment and their Swedish hunting rifles. He laughed when he wiped out a three-man team of them once. The poor bastards had never seen him. All they knew was that they were dying, one at a time. Then one night—the pain, the blackness, the hospital, Charlotte—it all came back to him in a flood of fear and agony. Instinctively, he touched the ugly wounds under his hat. He shook and began sobbing. The tears froze on his cheeks, and his nose began to run.

As he lay on his back staring at the stars, the fear and humiliation began to give way to a more recognizable emotion—anger.

"Why they doin' this to us, Mikey? They ain't got no call usin' that stuff. Shit, they think they're so damn smart. This here Ryker gotta die, old buddy. They gotta die too, don't they? It won't be like last time. We saw them first. They didn't see us, did they?"

His confidence began to return a little at a time. As

he lay there, he knew Ryker could be walking down the street right now.

Hayes quietly entered the small office where Ryker sat reading a newspaper.

"What the hell are you doing in uniform?"

Hayes looked embarrassed. "Hell, I don't know."

"Are you trying to be some kind of fucking martyr or something? Didn't you get your suits back from the cleaners?"

"I don't know. I just felt like . . ."

"Asshole. Give me the Beast," he said, as he stuck out his hand.

Hayes opened his tunic and produced the .357 Ruger Magnum. Ryker took it and stuck it in his belt.

"Call a fucking cab; I want to blow this joint," he said.

Hayes sat down and picked up the phone while Ryker went back to his newspaper. As Hayes spoke to the taxi dispatcher, Ryker looked up over his paper.

"Tell those clowns I want the cab *directly* in front of the funeral home. Tell them we have an invalid here or something."

As Hayes and Ryker waited for the cab, Cyrus rose unsteadily and peered over the parapet. Because he knew they were there, he could make out the two figures on the roof down the street without his scope. He wondered if there were any more.

The two shivering cops on the roof cursed the day they had volunteered for ESU duty. They expected a long, cold night ahead.

"Shit, I used to bitch about the heat in Nam," one of the cops said.

"You're an old fuck," the younger cop said. "Keep moving around to get your tired blood flowing. I'll scan for now."

They knew that the people in the apartment under them must be pretty pissed off about the noise, but they had seemed like nice people and, with any luck at all, they could get some hot coffee from them later. They took turns using their Starlight scopes, a few seconds at a time. A small two-way radio hummed at their feet.

Cyrus took all this in and decided that these two casual anti-snipers were not North Vietnamese regulars. He felt ashamed at having panicked. He reasoned that there couldn't be any more cops around—they would have picked him up an hour ago if there were.

The older cop stopped exercising and was scanning through his scope; as he swung the rifle in a horizontal arc, he stopped suddenly. He blinked and stared again, but he couldn't believe what he was seeing. He was looking right down the barrel of a rifle and scope less than two hundred yards away.

Cyrus fired twice. Both rounds struck the standing figure in the chest; he was dead before his body hit the roof. The younger cop stared in disbelief for a second longer than he should have. Two bullets buzzed past his ear. He dove head first onto the rooftop. He was torn between calling on the radio and avenging his partner's death before the sniper got away. Finally he grabbed his rifle and moved down the roof to the corner opposite. Carefully, he raised his head and brought the rifle over the parapet. The young anti-sniper didn't know where Cyrus was, but he tried to remember where his friend had been pointing his rifle before he was killed. Maybe that's where the killer was. He looked through his scope in the direction of the funeral home.

Cyrus was sweeping his rifle back and forth along the edge of the opposite roofline. He knew that the second cop, if he was any good, wouldn't appear where he hit the first one.

Suddenly, he saw the other cop. The cop spotted Cyrus at the same time and tried to steady his shaking aim.

One of Cyrus's bullets passed through the cop's Starlight scope and hit him in the right eye. The cop rocked backward on his haunches and dropped the rifle. He toppled slowly sideways and fell gently on his side.

Cyrus was shaking with the excitement of the kill. He had met an almost equal adversary and had beaten him. "Almost equal" in this game meant "dead." He smiled at his own cunning.

He waited, motionless, to see if the silent gun battle would bring any consequences from another quarter. He waited. Nothing.

Five minutes later, a taxi pulled up in front of the funeral home and honked. Ryker opened the door quickly and looked out.

"That asshole. He's across the street."

The cab was on the south side of the one-way street.

"Fuck it—let's move."

As the two men started quickly across the street, a car turned onto Ninety-fifth Street and passed in front of them; they were held back a second.

If he's here, he's seen us now, Ryker thought.

Cyrus looked down anxiously. Two men were heading for the taxi across the street. Was it Ryker or wasn't it? Why hadn't he thought about a taxi or a car? Cyrus started stupidly down at the long rifle with the mounted scope. Too close. Much too close. He picked up the rifle and turned on the scope. Too late to dismount it.

Hayes was tugging furiously on the rear driver-side

door. The driver-side windows, front and rear, were closed. The taxi driver looked around and motioned brusquely with his thumb to the other side.

Ryker pulled Hayes by the arm and began circling to the other side of the cab.

Without thinking, Cyrus stood straight up and watched as the two men tried to get into the cab. When they began circling the car, he had no doubt that the man in civilian clothes was Ryker. He raised the rifle and began twirling the adjustment knobs furiously. His targets were not more than fifteen yards distant. At this steep angle and at this close distance, aiming was going to be a problem. With his old scope, he would have had to aim very low to compensate for the false cross-hair center making this a tougher shot than one at two hundred yards. But with the Mark V, the computer adjusted, compensating automatically.

Ryker opened the door and grabbed Hayes by the arm, pulling him toward the open door.

He's sighting in on me, Ryker thought. *He's ready to kill me.*

The picture in Cyrus's scope was clear as a bell, considering how close he was. "Two dead sons of bitches are better than one," Cyrus said, looking at Hayes as he took a deep breath. His aiming point was Ryker's heart; he squeezed the trigger.

If he's here, he's got us zeroed by now, Ryker thought. *It's at least nine seconds since we left the funeral home.*

Hayes was in front of Ryker and bent down to enter the cab. Hayes raised his head and looked back at the funeral home. His eyes went up to the roof. He remembered.

Could we see it at night?

Yes, you could if you were looking in a direct line of sight down the tube from the sniper's end. . . . The other way is to look directly into the tube from the business end of the gun—by that time, the discovery won't do you much good though. Laughter.

It had *been funny,* he thought.

How far away can it be seen?

There's what's called a "visual security distance." That's the distance within which the light can be seen, head-on. I don't remember the distance, though. We'll find out.

At least fifteen yards or so, Hayes suddenly remembered. You could also see the flash from head on, despite the flash suppressor. He saw it now.

The bullet skimmed the taxi roof, passed through Hayes's larynx and severed his spinal column, deflecting slightly after it hit the hard bone. The partly spent bullet passed through the edge of Ryker's right pectoral muscle, between his arm and chest and buried itself in the building behind him. Both men pitched backward onto the sidewalk. Hayes's body was on top of his partner. His body jerked spasmodically, as his brain continued to send messages down his torn and ripped spinal cord. Their blood soaked into each other's clothing.

The taxi driver heard a sound as the bullet skimmed his roof. He looked up from his comic book and glanced over his shoulder. His two prospective passengers had disappeared. *Assholes,* he thought.

Ryker edged closer to the cab, with Hayes's body still on top of him. Painfully, he pulled the .357 Magnum from his belt and drew it between his and Hayes's body. When the gun was clear, he raised it toward the funeral home. There was little doubt in his mind that was where the killer fired from, but the cab partially blocked his view of the funeral home across the street.

The cab also blocked Cyrus's view. He considered

pegging a few shots through the cab, but he only had eight rounds left in his last remaining magazine. He waited, not knowing what to do.

The cab drew away. Ryker fired three times in quick succession at the blue light. The heavy Ruger bucked hard in Ryker's weakening right hand. The first bullet went high. The second bullet hit the brownstone parapet and threw a piece of it into Cyrus's face. The third bullet hit the rifle. The gun flew out of Cyrus's hands, hit him in the face and fell onto the parapet. For a split second it tottered there, then fell to the sidewalk below. The gun landed on its scope, and it made a loud pop as the air rushed into the vacuum of the long tube.

Ryker rolled painfully out from under the body of his dead partner and staggered across the street. He made a grab at the rifle as he passed it but missed. He pushed through the large oak door of the funeral home and slid across the marble lobby floor. The building was alive with running and shouting people as Ryker pushed past a group on the stairs and began climbing. He bowled over several people on the second and third floors. Without hesitating, he went up the last flight of stairs and pushed through the roof door. He shoulder-rolled across the roof three or four times with the Ruger in one hand and the Beretta in the other, but Cyrus was gone.

Ryker got to his feet and looked around. The buildings on both sides of the funeral home were five stories. He ran to the rear parapet. He could see Cyrus jumping a fence as he passed through the small backyards of the attached houses, heading west.

Ryker, bleeding heavily now, crashed down the back fire escape. His shoulder was throbbing and he wondered again if Cyrus had a hand gun, but he ran and hurdled the fences as though he didn't care if Cyrus were armed or not.

When he reached the end of the backyards, a large corner building loomed up in front of him. Cyrus was trapped in this last yard somewhere. Ryker crouched in the darkness.

Two shots rang out to his left. Suddenly, a thin shaft of light broke across the backyard. Cyrus had blasted the lock off a back door.

Sounds big, like a .45, Ryker thought.

Ryker went directly for the open door. He ran through the small lobby and through the open front doors. He stood on the stoop and looked up and down the street. Cyrus was walking quickly east on Ninety-fifth Street, back toward the funeral home. Ryker watched him for a second. He was less than a hundred yards distant, on the other side of the street, and he was out of range.

Ryker descended the front steps of the apartment house and began following at a walk. He was weak and out of breath. A large crowd had gathered around the body of Arthur Hayes. Cyrus walked around the crowd and crossed the street. As he did, he saw Ryker. Cyrus stood in front of the funeral home and looked around; Ryker knew Cyrus was looking for his rifle.

Fucking lunatic, Ryker thought, as he sped up.

Cyrus was still looking as Ryker got within seventy-five yards of him, then suddenly Cyrus turned and began walking east again. The street was filled with people now, and Ryker couldn't risk a shot. Cyrus knew this and took his time. He was exhausted and breathing hard.

As Ryker passed the spot where the rifle had been, he noticed it was gone. Someone must have picked it up. He glanced at the crowd that circled the body of his dead partner, trying to put the death of Arthur Hayes out of his mind. It wouldn't help anything to think about it now.

The two men continued east on Ninety-fifth Street. Neither had the energy to run; both knew that if they kept a hundred-yard separation there would be no shooting. Both had an ammunition problem. Ryker was concerned that Cyrus would try to force his way into a passing car or try to take a hostage. If he made a move in that direction, Ryker was mustering his energy to make a final sprint to close the distance. Ryker didn't care who Cyrus grabbed as a hostage. He wasn't going to play that game today, and he hoped Cyrus knew it.

Suddenly the night air was filled with the sounds of sirens. Ryker hoped that Cyrus would clear the block before the police cordoned it off.

As they walked, both men took stock of their positions. Ryker knew that Cyrus's .45 was a good weapon close in, but its disadvantage was its maximum effective range, which was only fifty meters. The Ruger was good up to sixty or seventy yards. Ryker realized that he had the decided advantage, although he had only three bullets left. Ryker dismissed the Beretta. At best, it would be good to make noise with, although it didn't even do that very well. He wondered how much ammunition Cyrus had left.

As they approached the end of Ninety-fifth Street at Central Park West, Ryker suddenly realized that Cyrus would head back into the park if he could. He had to keep the killer in sight and away from the park at all costs.

Ryker's chest was worse now. The bullet had passed through cleanly, not hitting the rib cage but, still, the pain was distracting. Worst of all, a stiffness was making its way down his arm. Ryker felt his grip on the Ruger loosening.

At Eighty-seventh Street, two walking policemen turned the corner onto Central Park West from the side street. They began walking north, toward Cyrus, and were less than fifty yards away. The killer spun around and looked for Ryker. He knew he was trapped. He caught Ryker's eye and looked back at the patrolmen who were closing on him. He began to draw his gun from his pocket. He looked back at Ryker, wondering what was the best way to make a stand. Then he saw something that sent a chill down his spine. Ryker was shaking his head vigorously and motioning with his hand. Automatically, Cyrus obeyed. He thrust the gun back into his pocket and moved into an apartment house alcove. The two patrolmen glanced at him for a second as they passed him.

Cyrus knew, and the knowledge raised the hair on his neck, that it was only him and Ryker now.

FIFTEEN

The two men continued walking. Cyrus had no doubt that they would walk for days if necessary, until one of them dropped from exhaustion. When they reached the Fifty-ninth Street Bridge, Cyrus turned and began walking on the pedestrian footpath. Ryker followed. About halfway across the bridge, above Welfare Island, in the middle of the East River, the footpath ended. Ryker and Cyrus faced each other at seventy-five yards. It was a classic stand-off. Both men drew their guns. Neither fired. They stood for a long minute.

"You didn't tell me this thing ended," Cyrus shouted.

"You didn't ask."

"I suppose one of us got to make a move."

Ryker didn't answer, and the men stood facing each other. It was almost nine o'clock, and the temperature on the bridge, with the wind whipping through the steel girders, was close to zero.

Ryker lit up a cigar. Cyrus stared at him.

When Cyrus saw a police car approaching from Ryker's rear he yelled, "Police." Both men crouched down. Ryker did the same when a squad car approached from the other direction.

The wind was getting stronger. Cyrus yelled above the whistling gale.

"Well, what do you reckon I ought to do?"

"Freeze to death, motherfucker."

"That's a bad way to go."

"Then jump."

"Worse yet."

They stood and waited.

Ryker knew that eventually Cyrus would jump onto the roadway and try to grab onto the back of a passing vehicle. He could see Cyrus eyeing the slower moving trucks as they went by at about forty-five miles per hour. Ryker also knew that the timing would have to be perfect. If Cyrus missed and fell, Ryker would be on him and shooting within seconds.

Ryker stood with his legs spread. He held the Ruger with one hand and had the other in his pocket. He barely moved a muscle.

Cyrus was starting to choke on his own mucous, and ice was forming around his watering eyes. He couldn't feel his feet anymore, and his hands were starting to throb.

Behind him, Ryker could hear the sound of a big tractor-trailer going through its gears. He knew it wouldn't be moving more than thirty miles per hour as it neared the crown of the bridge, where Cyrus stood.

As the truck came abreast of Ryker, Cyrus tried to look nonchalant. Ryker smiled at this bad acting. Cyrus was spring loaded to go; anyone could see it. As the truck came abreast of Cyrus, Ryker waved goodbye. Cyrus became confused when he saw that Ryker knew he was going to make for the truck. He got a false start and almost missed the rear bumper as he sprang after it. The driver didn't notice anything.

Behind the truck was an old Pontiac with a middle-aged couple in it. Apparently they liked the speed of the truck and hadn't bothered to pass it, or they were stuck behind it as the traffic in the outside lane shot past. Ryker ran behind the car, then jumped and landed on the trunk. The driver hit the brakes and Ryker, who was expecting this, held tight. He drew the big Ruger and waved the driver on. The terrified man began moving forward. He had seen Cyrus mount the rear of the tractor-trailer, and he knew from the movies that a chase was on. He didn't know who was the good guy, but the guy with the gun closest to him was definitely the boss. He followed the truck as it gained momentum on the down slope. Instinctively, he kept his distance. Every time he let the distance widen too much, Ryker tapped on his rear windshield with the gun. Eventually, the man got the hang of it. Ryker could see that Cyrus was trying to draw his gun. If he could peg a few shots at the Pontiac, the driver would panic and hit the brake or swerve. Ryker watched anxiously, but it looked like Cyrus's hold on the truck was too precarious for him to fire. Ryker considered firing himself, but the range was well over a hundred yards and the driver would probably go to pieces if he heard a shot. Just a few more seconds and they would be across.

On the exit ramp, Cyrus let go and rolled to the side. By the time he came to his feet, he realized that he had made a mistake. The car Ryker was riding on was less than fifty yards from him and closing fast. He turned and ran.

Ryker was trying to steady his aim, but on the bouncing car, he couldn't. The street was one pothole after another. He slid off the trunk and rolled to the side, got to his feet and ran.

When the distance was acceptable to both parties, they settled back into a walk. Cyrus knew that Ryker meant to walk him to death. For a wild moment, he even considered giving himself up to the first patrolman he saw. He was exhausted and frozen out of his senses.

Both men looked around at their new surroundings. The bridge had taken them to Long Island City in Queens. The area had once been industrial, but like the East Village, it was undergoing a kind of gentrification. Old loft buildings were being stripped to their steel girders and remodeled for artists, small advertising agencies, and new businesses that couldn't afford Manhattan's prices.

Although a few brave souls had moved into the residential lofts, the streets were deserted.

Ryker knew that Cyrus was torn between giving him the slip and killing him. But whatever he tried, he had to do it soon.

"Hey, Henry. You know why I beat up on your sister?"

No answer.

"Because she gave me a lousy blow job," Ryker yelled.

No answer.

"That little kid of hers looks just like you, Henry. Gettin' a little bit of baby sister, were you?"

No answer.

"Your friend, the nurse—Charlotte—said you were a fucking queer, Henry; said you were the worst lay in California."

Cyrus turned and faced Ryker. Ryker kept walking.

Seventy-five yards.

Both men drew simultaneously and fired. Ryker's

long barrel had the advantage at this range. Cyrus's .45 slug went wide, and Cyrus caught Ryker's .357 caliber bullet through his deltoid muscle, at the top of his right shoulder, near the base of the neck. Cyrus was knocked backward as the bullet passed through; Ryker fired twice again on the run and missed. Cyrus fired and Ryker hit the ground. Cyrus scrambled to his feet and ran. Ryker drew the Beretta and pegged two shots after him, but Cyrus was bobbing and weaving. Ryker got to his feet and began running as fast as he could, the Beretta in one hand and the empty Ruger in the other.

"You're a fucking loony, Henry. You're crazy. Kill yourself, Henry. You're too crazy to live."

Both men were on the point of collapse. Ryker's wound had coagulated, but Cyrus's was fresh and, as he ran, his beating heart sent spurts of blood through his opened shoulder. It felt warm and sticky.

Ryker's wound reopened with the exertion and he too started to bleed. The running men's footsteps echoed up between two huge factory buildings awaiting renovation. Both men were on the verge of going into shock, but Cyrus finally collapsed on his hands and knees and began to dry heave. His contorted mouth spit out bile and acid. Ryker took a dozen more steps and fell.

Both men began crawling painfully over the hard ground, through frozen dog feces and broken glass. After a few yards, Ryker staggered to his feet and began walking. Cyrus half-stumbled, half-crawled to keep ahead of him. He spotted an open staircase that ran up an old factory building and staggered over to it. He sat on the bottom stair and began to lift himself up, one step at a time, keeping the Colt trained on Ryker, who was about eighty yards away.

Ryker crouched behind a truck and caught his

breath. The factory buildings formed a horseshoe-shaped courtyard around the truck yard where Ryker was hiding. All the buildings had fire escapes or stairs leading to their rooftops. There was about five to ten feet between the buildings. Ryker ran and stumbled to the nearest building and began mounting the fire escape to the roof forty feet above. Cyrus spotted him and moved faster. Both men reached the roofs and tumbled over the parapets. Each of them lay breathing hard for a few minutes.

There were two buildings between Ryker and Cyrus. Ryker wondered if he could make the jumps between the buildings. As he lay on his back, he smiled and yelled, "Cy-russs!"

No answer.

"You cocksucker. You're going to suck the end of my Magnum before the sun comes up." The words echoed between the still buildings.

Ryker got to his feet and looked toward the building that the killer had climbed. The rooftops were a forest of ventilation shafts, skylights, and stairway huts. Ryker leaned on the parapet.

"Where's your big rifle now, asshole?" he shouted.

Silence. Then, "Go away."

Ryker laughed long and loud. A shiver went down the killer's spine.

Ryker shouted. "Is that the best you can do, Henry? You sister-fucker! Come and get me!"

Cyrus didn't like profanity, and he couldn't believe the things Ryker was saying to him.

"That all you know how to do—cuss? Can ya fight, big city boy? Come and get *me,* if you're so tough."

"I'll wrap your diseased dick around your ears when I get you."

No answer.

Ryker tired of the game. At least he knew Cyrus was

still there, and he doubted if the killer would come for him. Ryker walked, zombie-like, to the middle of the roof, turned around, took a deep breath, and ran. His left foot hit the top of the parapet and he sailed forward. As soon as he pushed off the parapet, he knew he wasn't going to make it. He stretched out his arms and grabbed at the opposite building. His right arm hooked the brick parapet. His wound began pumping blood again.

Ryker worked his way up and over the top, then collapsed in a large pool of freezing water and rolled over to a dry spot. He checked his guns and staggered to his feet.

Ryker stumbled to the other side of the roof and peered across to the last building separating him from Cyrus. This one was much closer. Rather than risk hitting the raised parapet from a running broad jump, Ryker stood on top of the parapet and made a stationary leap across. His stiff legs almost gave way under him. Again, he slammed into the opposite wall, not quite making it, and he had to hang from the parapet until he could muster the strength to pull himself up and over. With a final heave, he rolled over the parapet and fell to the roof. As he lay on his back, he picked up the Ruger that had fallen from his pocket. He wondered how he was going to make the last jump.

He didn't have to worry about it, though, because standing above him, smiling from ear to ear, was Henry Cyrus. Cyrus kicked the Ruger out of Ryker's hand and pointed his .45 at the cop's head.

"Why'd you say those things about my sister and Charlotte?"

"Just trying to be friendly," Ryker said.

"Think you're funny? . . ."

Ryker twisted his body and fired three shots from

the Beretta, through his pocket, into Cyrus's right shin. The sniper screamed and toppled as his leg gave out.

Ryker was on him in a second. He pulled the .45 out of the killer's hand by the barrel and slowly, methodically, because he was in no particular hurry anymore, knocked Cyrus's teeth in with the heavy gun butt. After he was satisfied that all of Cyrus's teeth were smashed, he rolled him over and stuck his fingers down the killer's bloody throat. Cyrus gagged up broken teeth, blood and mucus.

"We don't want you to choke to death, Henry. Someone might accuse me of police brutality—right?"

Ryker snapped a handcuff on Cyrus's right wrist and dragged him across the frozen roof to an electrical conduit pipe. He snapped the other end of the cuff around the pipe and frisked the semi-conscious killer. Ryker emptied Cyrus's pockets and stuffed the contents into his own.

The exhausted cop then cut a piece of cloth from Cyrus's coat with the killer's K-bar knife and tied a tourniquet around Cyrus's right leg, below the knee. He turned him over onto his back.

"Never had a prisoner bleed to death on me unless I wanted him to. What do you say about that? You thought I wasn't going to take care of you, didn't you?"

Cyrus groaned and blew bloody bubbles through his swollen lips.

"Speak up, Henry. Don't be mealy-mouthed. If you got something to say—say it."

Cyrus started to gag on his blood. Ryker sat him up and the broken man spat bloody hunks of his gums and coagulated blood down his chin. Ryker dropped him again.

Cyrus looked up at Ryker with dimming eyes. Ryker dragged himself over to a pool of frozen water, broke the ice and drank. He scooped up some water and ice, dragged himself back to Cyrus and rubbed it into the killer's face. He then propped himself up against an air duct and lit a cigar.

"You with me, Henry?"

A groan.

"Good, listen. You made a couple bad mistakes back there, boy. I guess you know what they were and I don't want to rub it in or anything—but you know what your big mistake was?"

Muffled groans.

"Can't hear you. Anyway, I pegged a couple of shots at you back there with this little Beretta. Now you should have been able to tell that wasn't the Ruger. Yet, you didn't know I had it when you got the drop on me. How's that?"

"Fugah."

"What? Fugah?"

"Fugaht."

"Forgot? Bullshit. You just couldn't tell the difference, you were so damned scared. You're out of practice, Henry. Too long in the loony bin."

"Fugah."

"Even if you did fugah, that was a serious mistake. A training mistake like that could cost you your life in an actual situation. Didn't they teach you that in the Army? They taught us that at the Police Academy. Shame."

More groans.

Ryker got up painfully and walked over to Cyrus. "You killed my partner tonight. What do you think I ought to do about it?"

Groan.

Ryker brought his heel down, with all his weight, on

Cyrus's testicles. Cyrus passed out. Ryker revived him with ice water. He walked over and retrieved his Ruger, then walked back to Cyrus. He stared down at the broken, bleeding body. The New York skyline was ablaze in the distance. After a few minutes, Ryker pocketed his two guns.

"Well, take it easy. I really have to be going." Ryker walked slowly to the fire escape.

Cyrus groaned loud. "Shumee."

Ryker was starting down the fire escape. He looked back over the edge of the parapet. "Shoot you?"

"Shumee. Pleece."

"Henry, I'm an officer of the law. I can't do that to a prisoner."

Cyrus let out a weak, pathetic wail.

Ryker smiled at him and said, "Freeze to death, motherfucker."